BLOOD OF THE BELOVED

Blood of the Beloved

Mary Coleman

iUniverse, Inc.
New York Lincoln Shanghai

Blood of the Beloved

iUniverse books may be ordered through booksellers or by contacting:

iUniverse
2021 Pine Lake Road, Suite 100
Lincoln, NE 68512
www.iuniverse.com
1-800-Authors (1-800-288-4677)

Because of the dynamic nature of the Internet, any Web addresses or links contained in this book may have changed since publication and may no longer be valid.

ISBN: 978-0-595-46405-0 (pbk)
ISBN: 978-0-595-70199-5 (cloth)
ISBN: 978-0-595-90699-4 (ebk)

Printed in the United States of America

2793 AD. This is a transcript of conversations following each of the lectures at the re-enactment symposium held on the subject of War. All texts are in the ancient English language of 2000 AD.

Each chapter begins with the abstract of the lecture the participants had just finished hearing.

www.BloodOfTheBeloved.com

dedicated to

Charles Hubert Coleman

my father

CONTENTS

Preface xi

Chapter 1: Introduction 1

Chapter 2: Violence by Individuals 5

Chapter 3: Violence by Groups 16

Chapter 4: War and Genocide... 25

Chapter 5: The Dance of Death 35

Chapter 6: Theories about the Causes of War 39

Chapter 7: Sacrificial Rituals 50

Chapter 8: The Blood of the Beloved 65

Chapter 9: Purity and Violence 76

Chapter 10: Shame Societies & Guilt Societies 89

Chapter 11: About men and war 98

Chapter 12: About Women and War 112

Chapter 13: War Substitutes for the Powerless................... 121

Chapter 14: Abandoning War by the Powerful 127

Chapter 15: Conclusion 141

Bibliography.. 151

Index... 165

Preface

Is it possible to stop the scourge of war or is it an intractable problem? Let's listen in on a *re-enactment convention* held in the twenty-eighth century A.D. This convention was held for historians and archeologists of that future century to review war and violence of the twentieth century A.D. and before that.

We shall be overhearing an archeology student and his professor discussing each of the lectures.

CHAPTER 1

▼

INTRODUCTION

Abstract 1001 Almost as soon as humans learned to write, they began describing war. Body counts and mounds of corpses were described as early as 2300 BC.

Leslie—Hey! Where were you sitting? I couldn't find you. Have you been to a re-enactment symposium before?

Irene—I was sitting in the rear; it's better on one's back. Yes, I've been to other re-enactment symposia about how people lived in ancient times. They have been on topics both serious and silly. It is interesting that this symposium on War is the one with the most participants so far.

Leslie—This first lecture began with an ancient version of an Iran-Iraq war that happened in 2300 BC—that was really a long time ago! Even back then, the winning king Rimish reported mounds of corpses heaped up—with 16,212 men killed and another 4,216 taken prisoner.[1] Was he exaggerating?

Irene—We have no way of knowing how overstated the descriptions and numbers were. So much of what was written in primitive times may not have been factual (in the sense we claim to use it today) but was full of those psychological hidden agendas found among political leaders. In this case, Rimish may been trying to intimidate by sheer terror. Some of the earliest recorded wars were around what was later called the Persian Gulf region.

Leslie—Is there any archeological proof of these ancient wars?

Irene—Yes, there is evidence even before wars were actually described in writing. A thousand of either round or oval-shaped clay bullets were found in a city in that same fertile crescent area. It was a city called Tell Hamoukar in Syria which was reduced to rubble about 3500 BC. [2]

Leslie—A thousand clay bullets so long ago! Did they eventually stop killing each other?

Irene—No; there were still going at it four millennia later. For example, in the Persian Gulf Region; three new wars were started in 1980, 1991 and 2003 AD. In fact, the 1980-1988 war was another Iran-Iraq War; it was one of those conventional wars of the bloody twentieth century, this time with 1 million lives lost, which ended in stalemate. The other two wars were waged inside Iraq.

Leslie—How do we know how many people Rimish's forces claimed to have killed in that ancient Iran-Iraq war of 2300 BC?

Irene—From a royal inscription found in a clay tablet archive. One of the first writing methods was a stick making marks on wet clay, producing a cuneiform script. The king Rimish was the son of Sargon, the famous ruler of Akkad credited with establishing the first recorded "world empire", which was located in Iraq.

Leslie—Who was Sargon?

Irene—Sargon was quite a character. Sargon probably was not his original name since it meant "the king is legitimate." The problem of legitimacy related to his birth; some sources identify his mother as a high priestess, but not necessarily of royal parentage. Her marriage seems to have been illicit, for after bearing Sargon in secret, she exposed him to the river in a reed basket. (The story resembles the story of Moses written more than a millennium later.) The baby Sargon was found by a water-drawer of the Euphrates River and raised to be a gardener.[3]

Leslie—If he was a gardener, how did he establish an empire?

Irene—When Sargon grew up, he managed to get the coveted job of cup-bearer to a king of Kish—perhaps through the influence of his mother. Kish was a Semitic-speaking city, that was an outpost in the extensive Uruk culture of the ancient Sumerians. Eventually Sargon rose to be a king himself, and then he conquered all the Sumerian city-states of his time. These were the first cities where much of what was referred to as civilization originally appeared. The Sumerians had invented the earliest writing system that caught on, and it spread to many cities with different languages, including Kish. As soon as that writing was developed to the point of telling a narrative, the clay tablets included descriptions of wars and lamentations by losers of wars and many other sacrificial activities.

Leslie—And what about Rimish?

Irene—Sargon was succeeded by his younger son, Rimish. The empire his son inherited was located mostly in Iraq/Syria but extended to some city-states in Iran—known as Elam in those ancient times. Rimish had to reconquer some of his father's conquests in Elam to continue to keep these eastern provinces inside the empire. It was in the province of Barahshun in Elam (Iran) that those mounds of more than 16,000 corpses were recorded.

Leslie—The Persian Gulf region must have been a very dangerous place to live for thousands of years.

Irene—Wars were not just limited to the Persian Gulf region. There was no end of killings in all the continents throughout primitive times; as soon as writing appeared in a society, there would be a description of wars. As populations expanded, the "mounds of corpses heaped up" grew larger and larger.

Leslie—So would you describe wars as mass murders?

Irene—That's a factual description. Over time the amount of blood deliberately spilled reached gigantic proportions—during the twentieth century, up to 100 million were killed during World War II alone. And wars were planned well in advance; in fact, in many very ancient cultures, there was a particular season each year for war. The Assyrians of the Near East went to war in the spring; the Kwakiutl Indians of North America had a summer season.

The Khmer Rouge who killed up to two million of their own people from 1975 to 1979 AD had a national anthem sung every day; it included this verse:

> Bright red blood
> which covers the towns and plains
> of Kampuchea, our motherland,
> Sublime blood of revolutionary men and women fighters!
> The blood changing into unrelenting hatred
> and resolute struggle,
> on April 17th, under the flag of the revolution,
> free from slavery! [4]

Leslie—"Bright red blood covering the towns and plains"—where do you find this kind of hate-filled material!

Irene—Calm down! You signed up for this symposium on your own. In any event, the next lecture is not about group killings; it is about individuals who killed during those primitive times; wars and genocides are later lectures. Actually this coming lecture should be interesting; there is an overwhelming amount of archival material on the subject of murderers in ancient times.

Leslie—Why are you looking at the last page of the re-enactment convention program?

Irene—I'm looking at a rather different point of view from the 20th century; there is a poem printed there:

> The woodland of slender elms,
> their broken trunks and limbs,
> sap spilled in the mud,
> earth that once held their roots
> submerged
> in
> the blood of the beloved.

CHAPTER 2

▼

VIOLENCE BY INDIVIDUALS

Abstract 1002 Most humans, who thrive on friendly social behavior and are programmed for empathy, need extensive retooling of their brains in order to murder. The individuals who do kill often have a combination of poor genetics plus maltreatment during childhood. When these psychopathic individuals become head of a criminal gang, their tendency toward murder is greatly amplified.

Leslie—That was a fascinating lecture. I've often wondered about murderers.

Irene—So, did you learn anything new?

Leslie—Well, actually, before this lecture I guess I shared the point of view of the primitive peoples. I did actually think that people killing each other was somehow inborn in human nature. However I didn't know such an attitude had a specific name: the *laisser-tuer* attitude.

Irene—(sighing) Unfortunately, if you look at primitive history, the misconception that "humans are natural born killers" can be easily understood. There was so much murder going on. Their history is replete with dramatic stories of individuals who murdered other people (*killers*), groups imitating the murderers (they called it *capital punishment*), groups deliberately setting up situations for their own members and members of other groups to be murdered (*wars*), and groups targeting groups in an attempt to wipe them off the map (*genocide*).

Leslie—This lecture was about single individuals who murdered other people. Will studying such individual killers help us fathom the historical mass murders called war and genocide that occurred in primitive times?

Irene—Perhaps only indirectly, because most individual murderers were outside the mainstream of primitive societies. It appears that group psychology rather than the psychology of individuals holds the key to those historical mass murders called war and genocide. In those situations, group affiliation itself altered the behavior of the individual members of those communities.

Leslie—If one reads documents from the primitive period, one gets the impression that many people were loners who later became murderers.

Irene—No, no! The overwhelming majority of people certainly were not murderers. We are descended from them; like us, the primitive peoples were social mammals, who preferred not to be alone. People were never cut out to be alone, not destined to be solitary individuals; being with other people is very crucial to the human species. Even back in primitive times, they knew that the best way to punish people was to put them into solitary confinement. The brain needs contact with others just as the body needs food.

Leslie—So the population in primitive times was more interested in socializing with each other?

Irene—Yes; it is a reality that we humans are a very social species of mammals. Since restraints on behavior are required for social living, we relate to each other by the processing of visual and social clues of people around us. We can "read" the most subtle movements of the 43 muscles of another person's face, giving us the ability to recognize and relate to the emotions of others. These clues allow us to act in a socially appropriate manner, to have feelings of empathy and expectations of reciprocity.

Leslie—So our *homo sapiens sapiens* species is programmed for empathy, not for natural born killing?

Irene—First of all, I object to using the term *homo sapiens sapiens* for people in the twenty-first century and before.

Leslie—Why? Weren't they our direct ancestors and people like us?

Irene—Yes, but the extra "sapiens" doesn't belong to people who go around killing members of their own species; it was a pretty dumb thing to do; it was a quite negative variant of vertebrate and invertebrate evolution. Just call them *homo sapiens* as the lecturer did; they were lucky to have that "sapiens" in their name at all.

Leslie—OK, but *homo sapiens* of the twentieth century, for example, were genetically programmed for empathy just like us?

Irene—We are all programmed for many things, but especially because we are a very social species, it is natural to be altruistic, to help rather than hurt[1]. Most children develop an innate sense of fairness that starts to become apparent as early as three years of age. Even back then, it was known that friendly social interaction induces an endocrine and metabolic pattern favoring the storage of nutrients and growth in humans. Empathy is a normal and healthy human behavior[2]; aggressive violence against other members of your same species, other human beings, is abnormal.

Leslie—But surely we are genetically programmed for aggression too.

Irene—Of course, aggression is critical to survival, but so is learning how to direct and suppress aggressive impulses[3]. Humans are complicated beings, not only are they programmed for empathy, they also suffer guilt if they hurt others.

Leslie—Alright, but if humans are programmed for empathy, how did the primitives get soldiers from one country to kill soldiers of another country during a war?

Irene—It wasn't easy. It was understood that in order to kill other people, most individuals had to have extensive retooling of the brain, a change of their reactions and thinking. So young people going into the armed forces of primitive times had to go through a basic training designed to turn them into killing robots.

Leslie—Did it work?

Irene—Not perfectly. Even after such extensive reprogramming, it was never a complete success. When soldiers were ordered to make a clear-cut murder as in a firing squad, one soldier would secretly be issued a blank bullet so that all the soldiers could think to themselves "maybe I wasn't the killer." There was a famous Christmas scene from the murderous trench warfare of 1915 in World War I. In that situation British soldiers deliberately played a soccer game with the enemy German soldiers explaining "We sheltered each other. Nobody would shoot at us when we were all mixed up." [4]

Leslie—If there was such ambivalence about killing each other, how did so many people get killed in those wars; the records show that a hundred million people worldwide were killed during the extended time of World War II.

Irene—It had to do with the length of the war and the number of people involved. But changes in weaponry was the vital clue. This problem of suppressing empathy in the twentieth century warfare became much easier after the soldier-killer was distanced from his victim (longer-range weapons) or even no longer visualized his victim at all (as in bombing from airplanes).

Leslie—So how was the *laisser-tuer* debate settled?

Irene—During the twentieth century, the human genome was first decoded and it was quite a humbling experience for these ancient people; for example, they discovered that fruit flies learn using the same genes that humans do. The debate about violence, the *laisser-tuer* debate, was called "nature versus nurture" as though they were separate entities. At first they didn't fully appreciate that no gene acts independently of an environment and that the environment always needs a genetic scaffold on which to act; after that concept was grasped, it was restated as "nature via nurture."[5]

Leslie—I'm not exactly clear on what "nature via nurture" means.

Irene—In terms of people who later became violent as individuals, it was that the person's specific genetic make-up did make some individuals more vulnerable to the effects of harmful experiences. This was particularly true of those with unwelcome changes (mutations) in certain specific genes.

Leslie—So were the people who killed, the murderers, considered to have genetic factors which set them apart from others?

Irene—In most cases, like any abnormal behavior, murder was a blend of both genetic and environmental factors. As historians now understand, murders in nonwar periods during primitive times occurred from individual killers who had an increased chance of an underlying genetic mental illness. Individuals who repeatedly harmed other people, both by violence and less dreadful means, had the label of *sociopath* or *psychopath*. In primitive times, the behavior of these individuals was often thought to be due to cultural or family factors. At that time, it was barely understood that this unusual kind of behavior had stable characteristics and was easily recognizable, both historically and cross-culturally [6]. This showed that such behavior had an organic basis [7].

Leslie—Alright, the manifestation of psychopathy could still be identified in completely different cultures. But didn't the environment—the family, the culture, the society—have something to do with people becoming murderers?

Irene—Yes, murders were more frequent in very hostile environments, particularly when the individual was toxic on drugs. Also murders were much more prominent when lethal weapons were lying around, in gun-toting cultures. However, in countries with low homicide rates in the twentieth century, such as Finland, it was found that people who murder or automurder as individual actors would have been considered in most cases as mentally ill and out of the mainstream [8]. And other special studies of pictures of the psychopaths' brains, called imaging studies, revealed reduction of brain substance and abnormal patterns of wiring between brain sections [9,10]

Leslie—So what kind of behavior disturbances are we talking about?

Irene—There was a very careful forensic study in another northern European country called Sweden that was written during the time when the group violence of war in that nation had stopped. The study found that 55% of the perpetrators of severe inter-personal crimes who *repeated* those crimes had childhood neuropsychiatric disorders—such as those causing learning disorders, the hyperactivity/poor attention syndrome, tics or autistic symptoms.[11] The investigators realized that there was a large genetic component to these brain problems. The same study reported that criminals who had committed only a *single* act of violence tended to have mental disorders of post-childhood onset.

Leslie—The fact that a mental disorder starts after childhood—does that mean that it does not have a genetic component?

Irene—Not at all. Many of the major mental disabilities, such as schizophrenia and bipolar disorder, have a later age of onset but occur in people who have underlying genetic risk factors.

Leslie—I do know that bipolar disorder means both manic behavior and depressive behavior.

Irene—This brings up the subject of depression and its relationship to violence. Where serious depression is associated with violence, genetic markers have been found. In the twentieth century, abnormalities in certain genes (the tryptophan hydroxylase gene and serotonin transporter gene) were found to be associated with violent forms of suicide.[12]

Leslie—Violent forms of suicide?

Irene—Some depressed killers would commit suicide after their spree of killing; they had too much intolerable suffering; in the end struggling with both depression and aggression destroyed them. In some families, an inheritable relationship can be demonstrated between homicide/suicide and a particular gene.[13]

Leslie—You can tell me that genes were associated with violence and suicidal behavior, but what I would like to know is what such killers were thinking.

Irene—There was a psychological theory that when the raw severe emotional pain was turned inward, it could cause physical symptoms in the body (somaticization) or induce thoughts in the brain of self-violence. However when the emotional pain was turned outward, it could result in violence toward others (perhaps hoping to kill the bad feeling in oneself by killing someone else).

Leslie—And a neurological theory?

Irene—In patients with impulsive aggression, it was known that there was decreased activation of the inhibitory regions of the brain [14]. These are the networks in the brain that dampen down, modulate, and balance out the networks carrying such thoughts of extreme action.

Leslie—Is there a genetic theory?

Irene—More or less, there are people genetically at risk for depression. Approximately half of all genes affect the brain, and genes form a lifelong interaction back and forth with the environment, which helps determine how they are expressed. The "epigenetic" factors are especially important to the brain in its early developmental stages.

Leslie—So what are you saying? Are you saying that the upbringing of these people who murder, the way they were raised, is a major or a minor contributor to their violent behavior?

Irene—As we discussed, deviant behavior is a mix of both genetic and environmental factors. There have been studies trying to tease out whether parents might be causing violence in children, also asking the basic question of how much cultural factors contributed to violence. There was a big research project prospectively studying children from birth to adulthood in three different countries, each living in a land with a different level of group violence (England, the United States, and New Zealand).

Leslie—So they were trying to predict which individual child might become violent as an adult?

Irene—Exactly. They measured both maltreatment during childhood and a genetic propensity to violence.

Leslie—What did they find?

Irene—It was so interesting. What the study showed was that 1) gender (being a boy), combined with 2) a gene (MAOA) associated with violence [15] and 3) maltreatment during childhood were the three factors needed together to produce an antisocial or violent adult. However in this study, *all* three factors were needed to produce a violent adult; two out of three of the factors was not enough. [16]

Leslie—How about the girls in the study?

Irene—It just confirmed what was already known; women commit very little violence compared to men [17]. In the communities studied during the twentieth century, women committed less than 7% of the murders.

Leslie—So you had to be a boy, maltreated during childhood and also with a particular gene, in order to be a violent adult in this study. The gene alone or maltreatment alone didn't do it?

Irene—Right; at least in that study.

Leslie—Alright, then how do you explain if an entire group of people begin regularly murdering (as armies do)—are they all mentally ill, at least temporarily? Is that what happened in primitive times?

Irene—No, that's not the explanation. When people are invested in a group to the point of losing their autonomy, almost anyone can become captive of a group identity which has murder as part of its ideology. Back then, this kind of groupthink and suppression of private doubts was considered an unfortunate but necessary part of life. The primitives accepted armies and group killing as inevitable from time to time.

Leslie—You mean the primitives thought just anybody could become a killer, given the necessary group identity and the necessary circumstances?

Irene—During the late twentieth century, there was an especially big debate about whether anybody at all, or "normal people" as they were called, could commit violence. After all it was observed that members of armies did many things, including very brutal murders, that normal individuals living at home could never even imagine. After World War II, a debate arose about whether any person at all, if thrown into the circumstance, could even participate in genocidal killing behavior.

Leslie—Surely no one believed that.

Irene—I'll give you the flavor of the debate about whether ordinary people could become murderers from a book written by Francois Bizot about a man called Duch [18]. Apparently Duch started out as "a revolutionary idealist smitten with the truth" and appeared to be a person just like any other. Duch saved Francis Bizot's life, yet later he became the director of a Khmer Rouge prison where *14,000 persons* were killed at his specific orders.

Leslie—14,000 people!

Irene—Historically, the Khmer Rouge takeover of Cambodia was an attempted genocide of one group of Cambodians by their fellow Cambodians. During the 1,364 days of Khmer Rouge rule, about two million people died as a result of their policies, calculated out to be 1,466 people dying each day. [19]

Leslie—1,466 people a day! These numbers are getting too much for me.

Irene—Yet Bizot believed that Duch was not predestined to be a killer, although there is evidence that Duch was a strange, reclusive child. [18] Bizot's book became part of the conversation among twentieth century thinkers that eventually led to our current understanding of the fantastic power of ideology in us humans with our deep need for group identity and approval, a power that often can suspend or cancel out our individual personalities, values and scruples.

Leslie—Surely it must be more than an ideology that can turn people into murderers!

Irene—Historically Duch became part of a criminal gang, which used ideology as its cover for its real agenda of mass murder. The gang became the powerful group identity of its members. Criminal gangs in primitive times were held together under the sway of a psychopathic leader. The role of the actual charismatic leader is a factor in taking any group into a killing spree, whether it is called war or genocide or whatever.

Leslie—So are you saying that psychopaths can not only be individual killers, but that they can control groups of people and lead them into murderous activity?

Irene—Yes, but only if the group of people is mentally prepared for the activity. A leader of one of the biggest criminal gangs in the twentieth century which used ideology as a cover [20] was a man called Stalin. As a young man, he raised funds for the Bolsheviks by robbing banks, mail coaches and steamships, and later became head of a powerful state. Although Stalin was not tested, it is possible that he had some variation of autistic-like symptoms because the second and third toes on his left foot were joined [21], and he had a phenomenal memory, likely that of a savant. He was said to spend his days reading lists of thousands of names of people to be punished or killed, a truly diabolical memory.

Leslie—I object to that comparison; savants can be wonderful, you know very well that savants have made major contributions to our peaceful modern society.

Irene—Yes, it is true; these geniuses have steered us away from war and many other miseries of primitive times, once they were properly appreciated and given an opportunity to put their minds to these supposedly intractable problems. To compare them to a monster like Stalin is quite offensive, but we can't rewrite history. There was an inability of primitive society to nurture and integrate these geniuses and use their brilliance in a positive way as we have done; in primitive times, savants occasionally used their brilliance for criminal activity.

Leslie—But, as you know, we in the modern age have learned pretty much how to prevent group violence and war, but are still struggling with how to identify in advance and take preventive measures for that rare individual who might become violent.

Irene—Yes, we are still dealing with an occasional murderer; that is a remaining frontier of knowledge. Fortunately, criminal activity arising just from economic deprivation is now a thing of the past. And today even the hard-core of potential criminals—such as those children with the homicidal trio (late bowel training, fire-setting and killing of small animals)—tend to be in trouble early and thus, in most cases, can be intelligently steered during adolescence into nonviolent lives.

Come on; it's time for the next lecture; this one is not about violence by individual people, but about violence by large groups of people back in those primitive times.

CHAPTER 3

▼

VIOLENCE BY GROUPS

Abstract 1003 Groups, which have their own rituals, rules of behavior, history and relationship to other groups, also have their own way of thinking which is specific to that community. In primitive times when circumstances deteriorated, there could be a shared sense of depression, enhanced by a charismatic leader. One way of dealing with these shared bad feelings was aggressive violence in the form of war.

Leslie—We are sitting through a war symposium, yet the last lecture about mentally ill people has turned out to have its limits when you are trying to study war.

Irene—For sure. One did not need a medically abnormal brain—with its anatomical variation or its disrupted biochemistry—to kill in primitive times. It certainly is not sufficient to explain the violence of war. In the end that could be only explained by studies of group behavior; that is, the history of the so-called "normal" people.

Leslie—So the relationship of depression and violence, as seen in individuals, is not that relevant?

Irene—It does have some relevance, but with the caveat that community depression is environmentally based (culturally based); it is not due to a particular group of people being biochemically at risk for depression. Any individual can feel depressed when very adverse things happen in her life or to his group. And history does suggest that it is not just each individual who undergoes depression alone; entire groups of people can actually undergo what might be called "political depression" all together, secondary to some adverse political/economic event that affects them all.

And, as is characteristic of the state of depression, there can be a lot of shared regressive thinking among them at that time.

Leslie—I don't understand how that would happen. How could an entire group of people undergo a community depression together?

Irene—Usually it requires a charismatic leader to take advantage of a depressed society, and make its members even more depressed and angry as they share those feelings together. This is done by forcefully emphasizing the group's losses, sometimes even if they happened a long time ago. In those cases which emphasize historical losses, there is a Binion concept called *traumatic reliving*. Such leadership can push a depressed group down very treacherous roads indeed.

Leslie—But if the contemporary and historical losses of a group are emphasized, doesn't that make them feel like victims? Now just what does that accomplish?

Irene—You are right; it can become a shared historical victimization. A twentieth century psychiatrist, Vamik Volkan, described this as a desperate psychopolitical ploy to enhance the group identity of all its members.[1]

Leslie—I don't get it. Why would a depressed group of people think it would enhance their group identity to feel like victims?

Irene—I suppose it is something like no longer being depressed alone, having your distressed feelings accepted and shared and even making you more tightly part of your group. You are no longer suffering alone; you are all suffering together. Remember group identity is such an important part of one's identity; we are such social animals.

Leslie—So if groups of people get very depressed together, do they react like individuals and start thinking about aggression?

Irene—Indeed. Groups whose thoughts are synchronized by depressive group fantasies often tend to turn their bad feelings outward into murderous aggression toward other groups. Occasionally, in extreme circumstances, they might even turn their aggression inward towards themselves in massive suicides.

Leslie—Murderous aggression, massive suicides—what are you talking about?

Irene—In primitive times, the intimate relationship between suicide and murder wasn't that well understood, often for the individual and most certainly for the group. Death was everywhere in these cultures; in many societies, the normal tendencies for empathy and generosity were twisted beyond recognition.

In primitive times, it was considered a very noble thing to voluntarily be willing to die for one's country or for one's ideology (to be sacrificed).

Leslie—Surely you aren't saying that voluntary suicide was a part of ancient group cultures?

Irene—It depends on how you define it. In some group situations, overt suicide became an acceptable alternative. In all war situations, suicide is a possible outcome in anyone who joins an army; they wouldn't die if they stayed home. If one understands the relationship between suicide and murder, it could be noticed that the patriotic idealists entering armies willing to kill were also willing to die. Young men would volunteer for armies, hoping to be part of the killing side of the agenda, but accepting the possibility of their own death in battle.

Leslie—Death in young men; that is very sad indeed.

Irene—As you and I know only too well, even today humans have a fascination with death; the fascination itself hasn't disappeared with our present peaceful society. In primitive times, historians were particularly focused on wars (mass murders). Gory excesses of group murder dominate the history books written during primitive times. And even when individual and group homicidal killings were diminished, the fascination with gore and murder would continue in other forms. The British murder mysteries were very popular in their time yet they came out of an island nation with one of the lowest murder rates in the world.

Leslie—Did the British, with their low murder rate, also give up group killing (war) during the twentieth century?

Irene—No, like in most other counties at that time, wars continued, with excuses for them as numerous as the human imagination could create. Remember wars didn't happen out of the blue; they were cooperative efforts by the group; they were psychologically and militarily prepared for in advance. Often the final up-front excuse to get the killing going was that one's group was being attacked, sometimes faked by the leadership. To those involved, once the war started, it no longer mattered which side one was on and whether your side had decided to attack, i.e. start the sacrificial ritual first.

Leslie—So, in primitive times, was it understood why groups of people behaved that way?

Irene—Back then, thinkers began studying the psychology of groups of people.[2] It was known that since humans are such social animals, the formation of groups is elementary to the human condition. In those times, there was a huge debate about whether a group has its psychology based on the individual psychology of its members, or was more than that. The question would be phrased: is group psychology just a summing up, or is it a distinctive and apart from the blend of all the individual psychologies.

Leslie—So what answer did they come up with?

Irene—At first there was a so-called Lockean theory of social groups as aggregations of autonomous individuals. Later it came to be understood, as it is today, that groups of people are a separate ontological entity that includes behavior not always derived from the laws of individual psychology.

Leslie—A separate ontological entity? Pretty fancy language.

Irene—All it means is that each group once formed becomes an entity to itself, quite often a long-term body which not only outlasts its individual members, but also transcends them. The group develops its own rules of behavior, its own history, its own rituals and its own relationship to other groups. It may have its own special language, customs, foods, and clothes.

We know that groups develop shared images and symbols that have their own special group autonomy; they are used in rituals which exist to strengthen the particular identity of the group.

Leslie—All I ever learned about groups was that they shared cultural myths.

Irene—Yes, these are the stories of the group, which become part of the shared identity of its members. One of the most interesting characteristic of group myths, which is also found in biological systems, is that when the underlying subject is the same, apparent opposites could have very close or identical meanings.

Leslie—What does that mean?

Irene—In biological systems, for a compound to be above or below the so-called normal range can often result in very similar or identical symptoms in the patient. In group myths, there appears to be a similar characteristic—apparent opposites can have close or identical meanings.

Leslie—Do people need to have those group myths; can humans survive alone?

Irene—It is almost impossible. Groups meet the basic human needs; that is why they are found in all societies; they are the key to survival. Besides sheer physical survival, they meet the human need for social communication, the need for a general identity, the physical pleasure of being in tune with others, for relief of daily boredom and even for the hope that one will be institutionally remembered after one's death.

Leslie—So humans must become submerged into their groups?

Irene—Something like that; they become members who share the ideologies and fantasies of their society. To the extent that people become members of their group, they add a layer of new identity. This community identity (the cap and coat) can be on top of their family identity (their underlying clothes) and their personal identity (their underwear) and, in some situations, can actually conceal and obscure their underlying individuality.

Leslie—Don't people get their ideologies and fantasies from their families?

Irene—Yes, but the families are part of a society. It is more than just the family passing on the local customs to the growing child. As one writer in primitive times put it, individuals absorb their group culture all their lives long, through ever present "cognitive templates". [3] These are stored outside the individual through many and various cultural means, including specially shared language.
These templates, these aspects of a culture, can be detected many generations after they first appear. One example was The Day of the Dead pageants in Mexico, which reflected the ancient Aztec bizarre focus on death many hundreds of years later. Fortunately, the nine principles of Nazi ideology, as deciphered by Gonen[4], after some back and forth eventually disappeared in later German culture.

Leslie—Yes, it is known that cultures can continue patterns for generations and tend to be conservative . But are you implying that the members of groups tend to think alike?

Irene—Not exactly; every human has many original thoughts. However, in times of community crisis like war, people can suspended their autonomy as persons with their own individual sense of limits, of right and wrong, of appropriate behavior, and become overwhelmed by the group's concerns and answers.

Leslie—So what happens when they all start to think alike?

Irene—In certain special situations when individuals are participating in a group activity, their minds can actually become aligned. This can be seen most clearly when the group is physically in one place, but the same phenomenon can be observed developing even when there is only remote contact, such as the internet chat rooms of primitive times.

Leslie—That doesn't seem right to me; I know I think as an individual. I wouldn't be influenced by a crowd.

Irene—Are you sure? Although humans believe that they are rational individuals who think for themselves, when in a crowd, they tend to get caught up by the group psychodynamics and become influenced by the consensus opinion of the group. And simply by physically living in a particular community, it has long been known that groups tend to share a set of "hegemonic beliefs and fantasies"—meaning that such community ideas enjoy a presumption of truth that ceases to be routinely evaluated by the group.[5]

Leslie—What kind of truths?

Irene—In the past, this failure to evaluate a factual truth about challenged shared beliefs was especially prevalent in war situations. For example, during the twentieth century war in Bosnia, whole Bosnian populations were terrorized, civilians interned on a massive scale, hostages tortured and summary executions were common—yet the Serbian people, whose forces were committing these very atrocities, actually believed that they were a small, heroic country being horribly and unfairly victimized. [6]

Leslie—But in those war situations, it was the soldiers who commit the atrocities.

Irene—Yes, but the soldiers are individual members of the group who are acting out the group's violent message, no matter how dark and horrible it is. On behalf of their group, they felt quite free to commit acts they would never even consider for a moment as private persons; their actions were "in the name of the group." When they committed murder on behalf of the group as instructed by the leader (father of the group), they were applauded for it, felt exuberant about it, and even proudly wore medals commemorating their murders. Yet the overwhelming majority of them would never, never commit murder as private individuals and would be horrified if such a scenario was even suggested.

Leslie—They wore medals commemorating murders? No.

Irene—Regular, intermittent war was a characteristic of most of the societies seen in primitive history; the surviving warriors after each conflict would be given rewards, including medals to wear on their chests. These medals were displayed near the nipple area, as if they had nourished society with the milk of human kindness!

The historical pattern was of intermittent war, broken by periods of temporary peace. A group would "twin" with a potential adversary and after that conflict was finally resolved, they sooner or later would "twin" with the same or a new enemy. A historian of primitive times called this "the need to have enemies and allies"[7]. Certainly the unending need of most groups for the intermittent violence of war jumps out of the history books of the primitive period. Here is what one twentieth century thinker who experienced the Holocaust thought:

> Perhaps for reasons that go back to our origins as social animals, the need to divide the field into "we" and they" is so strong that this pattern, this bipartition—friend/enemy—prevails over all others. Popular history, and also the history taught in schools, is influenced by this Manichaean tendency, which shuns half-tints and complexities; it is prone to reduce the river of human occurrences to conflicts, and conflicts to duels—we and they. [8]

Leslie—When did this horrible pattern start?

Irene—As far as we can tell, early in the development of *homo sapiens,* as social considerations became prominent, the intense experience of impacting life by killing other humans was taken over by the group. Each group had its own murder monopoly; individuals were not supposed to act on their own.

Here is a sonnet about *traumatic reliving* by Rudolph Binion, the twentieth-century historian who suggested that this powerful concept, which was originally developed for individuals, applies to groups of people:

> No traumas get forgotten, big or small.
> The ones you manage to put out of your mind
> In their entirety, or to recall
> With the traumatic affect left behind,
> Are thereby ready to revisit you
> In actuality, to be replayed
> By you in thin disguise, to recur through
> A proxy with that affect overlaid.
> You wince remembering a twist of fate
> That caught you short, a loss that wiped you out,
> A death you caused, a love turned to hate,
> A shameful episode you brought about?

Be glad such misadventures fill your head:
That way you won't recycle them instead. [9]

CHAPTER 4

▼

WAR AND GENOCIDE

Abstract 1004 War was practiced throughout primitive times; as soon as narrative writing was invented, it described wars already well developed. War, which appeared to be about boundaries and power, actually was a planned ritual of human blood sacrifice. Civil wars, in particular, resulted in massive amounts of human blood sacrifice. Genocides were facilitated by war, particularly the purity types of genocides.

Leslie—That was some lecture! Were there really that many wars during primitive times?

Irene—Unfortunately, yes. Almost all groups had intermittent periods of hostility toward other groups which would lead to full-fledged wars. They were called the zigzags of history—war, nonwar period, next war, nonwar period, next war, on and on.

Leslie—What would determine when the next war began?

Irene—It depended upon the historical circumstances, but in general it was when the sacrificial protective effect of the previous war was psychopolitically used up. There is a whole lecture coming on the sacrificial effect of those wars.

Leslie—In history when did wars begin?

Irene—We have no idea. As soon as writing was invented, the very earliest writing shows that war, as practiced throughout that primitive period, was already developed and perfected in endless detail. The first narrative writings of the Sumerians, who began writing on clay tablets, are full of descriptions of city-states fighting other city-states in wars. These early writings also contain a heart-rending literature of lamentation by the losers of those conflicts.[1]

Leslie—So wars were well underway even before they were first recorded?

Irene—Clearly; I can't answer your question about when wars actually started, replacing what may have been even more primitive genocidal behavior. Many ancient cultures vanished, often through violence. When one group had the ability to destroy the other group, then genocide would occur; war probably occurred when two groups became somewhat more equal in power.

Leslie—Are you saying that war replaced genocide?

Irene—No, no. I don't want you to misunderstand that genocide disappeared with the advent of war; rather genocide continued as an integral part of many wars right through the end of the primitive period. One thing that can be shown, at least during the time period when we have written records, was that the genocides involved a number of the same elements as war.

Leslie—Which were?

Irene—Targeting and demonizing another group of people when planning in detail *well in advance* how to defeat or destroy them. With genocide, the purpose was to totally eliminate the enemy peoples. Believe it or not, war was thought by some primitive thinkers to be an advance, since its purpose was just to defeat and exploit enemy soldiers, not totally destroy the rest of the population.

Leslie—You talk about preliterate cultures; but I thought that the twentieth century was very genocidal.

Leslie—It was. There was slaughter of the Armenians, Jews, Cambodians and Rwandans. Two of the ancient peoples who were able to survive extinction in the Mediterranean world of antiquity—the Jews and Armenians—lived on as cultures for over two thousand years only to be targeted for genocide in the bloody twentieth century.

Leslie—The lecturer spoke of the Rwandan genocide as an average of 8000 murders a day. Surely that wasn't correct!

Irene—The records show the killing of 800,000 people in the course of 100 days.[2] The Rwandan genocide was not random; much of it was planned by the government with lists of the names and addresses of the victims prepared in advance. The Washington Post reported that "the heads and limbs of victims were sorted and piled neatly, a bone-chilling order in the midst of chaos that harked back to the Holocaust of the Jews."

Leslie—Why did the lecturer focus on the Rwandan genocide?

Irene—Possibly because it demonstrated the principle of how group identity may trump absolutely everything. In the case of two Roman Catholic nuns of the Benedictine order, their ethnic identity of being Hutu overrode religious ideology, gender, education and a single drop of altruistic compassion.

These nuns were besieged by up to 5,000 Tutsi civilians, mostly women and children, seeking sanctuary in their convent from Hutu killers. The nuns not only refused sanctuary, but informed the Hutu militia where the Tutsis were hiding. Sister Maria Kisito has been accused of providing jerry cans of gasoline that the death squad used to set fire to a garage in which 500 persons were hiding.

Leslie—Enough! Why was there so much discussion of genocides in a lecture about war?

Irene—Because in so many ways, the presence of a war facilitated genocides. For one thing, weapons of murder were more readily available. In the midst of so much war killing, any political will to protect minorities and helpless civilians was deeply eroded. The last hope of the victims, outside observers who might try to intervene to stop a genocide, were prevented from entering or staying in the area by the presence of a violent war going on. Outside political forces, unable or unwilling to make a distinction between the forms of ritual sacrifice, often used the war as an excuse to do nothing, citing the evidence that it was unclear as to which killings were war-related and which were deliberate genocidal killings.

Leslie—I didn't fully accept the concept in the lecture of two different kinds of genocides—territorial genocides (acquisition of territory/wealth) versus purity genocides (cleansing of non-homogenous impure people from a population). It seemed to me that the two different types of genocide overlapped a great deal.

Irene—That's a good point; they did overlap in major ways. In the case of territorial genocides, whole continents were seized when the native American tribes and the Australian aborigines were destroyed, yet there is no doubt that "racial" purity factors helped rationalize those wholesale destructions of these people, their languages, and their cultures.

Leslie—And conversely, how about purity genocides, weren't there territorial aims of the collection of land and wealth associated with them?

Irene—Yes, for example in the Nazi Holocaust, the Germans seized property, goods, clothes and guards even collected hair, teeth and skin from the gassed bodies in the extermination camps.

Leslie—So if the two types of genocides overlapped, what was the difference?

Irene—In the territorial genocides, there remained an element of chance, of accident, of death by disease or starvation rather than overt murder. Not so in the purity genocides; they were usually planned just as wars are planned. The Nazi killers were an example of the horrifying behavior that can become acceptable "in the name of the group"—bizarre sadistic fantasies acted out without fear of sanction, indeed as a source of Nazi group esteem.

Leslie—I simply don't understand how purity genocides in particular could possibly happen.

Irene—It *is* almost impossible to imagine. I'll tell you one theoretical construct about it, but don't know if it is right. Genocide is the most extreme form of group violence. One theory is that the impulse to wipe out one's own family, particularly your own parents and rival siblings, is a deeply shared hidden feeling with others in the group and thus can be acted out together on someone else's family.

The perpetrators of this kind of violence appear to be very depressed people, troubled by violent suicidal fantasies themselves. But they project the violence away from themselves onto a vulnerable minority in their midst. It is all one big "family", members of the minority are sufficiently integrated into the larger group so that they can serve as human substitutes, human scapegoats. In such situations, the more integrated the minority is with the majority, the more eligible they become as genocidal victims when the political situation calls for human sacrifice.

Leslie—But isn't the leadership responsible, with the actual killers just following orders? Not everyone in a group can be that depressed.

Irene—Not everyone of course, but plenty enough people to share the group fantasy of hatred and depersonalization of the victims. In the case of the Nazis, although there were special troops specialized in committing the genocide, regular soldiers also participated in murdering civilians in Jewish communities.

Leslie—Hatred and depersonalization sounds like preparation for a war. I suppose it is a matter of degree.

Irene—That's one way to look at it.

Leslie—So how about the theoretical construct about wars. Was it the same?

Irene—Well, we have many different layers of theory and information on wars during primitive times. At first look, wars of the primitive era appeared to be about boundaries and power.

Leslie—Boundaries and power—that certainly would explain a lot of history.

Irene—*Homo sapiens* behavior in a group is so strikingly different from other animals. Since humans appeared to have a more advanced intelligence than other mammals, it was a great puzzle why humans were so much more destructive in their group behavior, killing each other over boundaries and power.

Leslie—So much more destructive?

Irene—Yes, of their environment for example. The first actual city constructed by humans was Uruk in ancient Mesopotamia about 3500 BC and it gradually destroyed all the crop land around it until it lost its power. Humans didn't learn, and just kept destroying the environment for many millennia after that.

Leslie—But wouldn't you argue that the greatest destruction of primitive times was by wars, that is, wars about boundaries and power?

Irene—Very good. With the invention of nuclear weapons, primitive peoples reached the peak of their destructive effect. They combined war and environmental destruction, even rendering portions of land so radioactive that it became uninhabitable.

Leslie—So that certainly doesn't sound very intelligent if they kept inventing weapons of war to kill each other and destroy their own living space. Why did they continually go to war over boundaries and power?

Irene—Alright; here's a postulated theoretical construct on why they were so different from other mammals. In the twentieth century, a few thinkers noted that the very first issues confronting an infant soon after birth are the boundary between himself and his mother, and the power to control his mother.

Humans are different from all other mammals in that after birth, it takes about two months before a baby can move against gravity; he must be lifted to the breast. All other baby mammals can find the breast on their own. But the infant's mind is not idle during this two month period of such helplessness. At birth, the infant is interested in the mother's face, she is already learning and thinking at a phenomenal rate. In fact, the younger the baby, the faster the rate of brain metabolism.

Brain growth is greatest in the months after birth and gradually decreases with age; this means that humans have their greatest amount of brand new learning when they are essentially helpless infants.

Leslie—I thought we were talking about war being fought over boundaries and power.

Irene—We are. The first issues that a baby has to think about is boundaries (being separate from the mother's body) and power (the development of an antidote to helplessness.) So there was a theory which postulated that war might be the reliving of the initial infantile issues—that is, boundaries and power.[3] It was might have been what made humans so different. In order for war to happen, there was no question that it involved thought regression to much earlier simple and irrational ways of thinking; this was the argument.

Leslie—But other mammals, which don't go through such a period of infantile dependence, are also interested in boundaries—for example, wolves used their scent to mark the boundaries of their territories.

Irene—Yes, animal group behavior is covered in a later lecture. I didn't say the theory was complete or even right. Psychologists in primitive times did create a concept called *psychogeography* which explored what external geographic features might have symbolized in terms of internal intrapsychic boundaries [4].

Leslie—That's too fancy for me. Alright, whatever caused it, we can agree that to the observers in primitive times, boundaries and power appeared to be the overt purposes of most wars.

Irene—The overt purpose, yes. But the covert purpose, as we think today, likely was an entirely different matter. That covert purpose remained no matter what the stated purpose of a war was, including some wars at the end of the primitive period where there were no apparent territorial (boundary) aims.

Leslie—So what was the hidden purpose?

Irene—The historical data is very clear that war was an exercise in mass murder planned in advance. Groups went to war knowing that, in addition to enemy soldiers, many of their own soldiers would be killed.

Leslie—I thought the purpose of war was to kill the enemy.

Irene—Although the propaganda of wars placed an emphasis on killing the enemy, we now know that groups planning a war actually were planning a deliberate killing spree of their own soldiers. There were a number of examples during World War I where the hidden plan became overt. In France when soldiers refused to charge into deadly machine gun fire, Marshall Pétain ordered that a random selection of the soldiers who had mutinied were to be shot within 24 hours without a trial. In Russia, soldiers were ordered into battle without enough ammunition, sometimes without every soldier even having a gun.

Leslie—What! Soldiers going into war without even having a gun to fight with!

Irene—Another example of deliberately killing your own soldiers from World War I is the ordering of soldiers into hostile machine gun fire only half an hour before the Armistice took effect which ended that war. The cease fire had been signed at 5:00 a.m. and was official at 11:00 a.m. on Nov 11, 1918. Nevertheless soldiers from the U.S. 26th Division fighting in France were ordered into lethal German fire at 10:30 a.m. [5]

Leslie—That's unbelievable!

Irene—The soldiers actually caught in these life-threatening situations tried to minimize their own casualties, but often it was too late; their societies deliberately placed them in harm's way. The official line of each military was that the purpose of war was to kill enemy soldiers and spare their own soldier's lives. The soldiers would struggle hard to save their own lives and those of their buddies. But they could not overcome the true agenda—some of them were destined to die.

Leslie—So just entering the army at all was very dangerous; it was playing with life and death; with the chance of dying.

Irene—Yes, there was a significant chance of dying, it was preplanned. It should be noted that these wars were not prepared as random killing sprees; they were usually targeted killing sprees of the late adolescents and young adults, mostly male, and mostly lower ranking soldiers who were actually exposed to hostile fire. When, during the late twentieth century, guns became lighter in weight so they could be carried by children, then boys also were kidnapped or forced into becoming tiny soldiers.

Leslie—What are you saying?

Irene—That such group-planned targeted killing sprees of members of a society has another name—it is called *a ritual of mass human sacrifice.*

Leslie—No! Isn't it true that rituals of mass human sacrifice were only found in the very early societies?

Irene—That is not correct; I'm sorry, but sacrifice never stopped. Throughout the primitive period, human sacrifice just gradually became more disguised and covert. War became a fiendishly clever deceptive way for a society to practice mass human sacrifice of their own young men.

Leslie—That doesn't make sense to me; I always thought that the purpose of war was to kill the enemy soldiers, not one's own soldiers.

Irene—Wars were so horribly cunning because the society got its partner in death—the other group that the society was fighting—to do the sacrificing for it. Each side in a war situation killed the young men of the opposite side. Thus each side practiced mass human sacrifice on behalf of its opponent. This appeared to be the hidden secret deal between the war opponents.

Leslie—You haven't convinced me.

Irene—Well, let's take a step back. You know that in the case of human sacrificial rituals, in order to be eligible as a human sacrifice on behalf of a group, the victim had to be a member of the group itself. Strangers wouldn't do.

Leslie—Yes, I know that.

Irene—So where was the focus of the group? Which group of soldiers had their numbers exactly counted? Which group of soldiers were ritually mourned and had monuments built to them? It wasn't the enemy soldiers.

Leslie—Well there would be body counts of the enemy during a war, as we heard in the first lecture.

Irene—Yes, commanders in the field would brag about the number of enemy exterminated, but these killings were almost immediately forgotten. The society was instead intensely focused on the deaths of its own soldiers.

Leslie—What about the soldiers who survived?

Irene—The insane violence of war forever branded its participants. Although many soldiers bravely insisted that they were proud and happy about their experiences in the armed services and suppressed their negative reactions, in truth many were often traumatized by what they did and what they saw. Even if they didn't get killed, many soldiers had been through the numbing experience of being "chosen" for possible death by their own society; their postwar lives were forever altered. Like those who remain alive after participating in any killing field, many suffered from survivor guilt. One could even make the argument that post-traumatic stress was a normal reaction by soldiers to such highly abnormal experiences.

Leslie—I'll have to think more about this. What about civil wars, when both sides belonged to the same group entity?

Irene—In primitive times, there were a lot of civil wars. They would become one gigantic sacrificial ritual for the groups, because there is a double mass sacrifice inside the same nation. Civil wars in general tended to be extra bloody as brothers killed brothers. The Battle of Marston Moor, 1644 AD, in the English Civil War had the largest number of soldiers ever fighting on English soil, leading to the largest communal burial ground in that land.[6]

Leslie—I guess you would call that burial ground a human blood sacrifice site, perhaps even a double sacrifice site.

Irene—Good point. Now it's time for the next lecture where we learn how wars actually got started in primitive times.

CHAPTER 5

▼

THE DANCE OF DEATH

Abstract 1005 No matter how it appeared, war never occurred out of the blue. There was a deliberate built-up of arms and political preparation of the populace. This dance of death occurred between two groups, focused on each other like addicted lovers, in the period of preparation for war.

Leslie—That was some interesting lecture; how hypocritical the primitive people were as they prepared for war in advance, yet talked the talk of peace!

Irene—Yes, we have now documented that virtually all societies in primitive times went to war on a periodic basis, but surprisingly have also found that some of these very same groups of people apparently struggled hard to obtain peaceful solutions. In fact, there was a lot of peace talk before each war in the twentieth century; apparently the reason for the wars increasingly had to be disguised. In fact, before the in-depth study was begun, at first we were rather surprised at how war seemed to pop out rather suddenly from an otherwise rather peaceful society in primitive times. But this was not the way it worked at all. War did not come out of the blue. There were always elaborate preparations and telltale signs.

Leslie—How could you tell if war was coming?

Irene—It worked this way—it was like a courtship, the two opposing group started focusing on each other. It took two to have a war; it was the slow sinuous Dance of Death. Both sides were involved even if it appeared on the surface that one side or the other was the sole instigator, the apparent planner of the war. In fact they were each other's preselected targets.

Leslie—I thought "dance of death" referred to 14th century European horrors, such as recurring famines, the Hundred Years War and the Black Death.

Irene—Yes, and Dance of Death had many later uses. *Totentanz* was a piece of evocative music by Franz Liszt, *Dödsdansen* was the title of a play by August Stringberg to characterize a man and his wife ritually tormenting each other, and there were a number of Dance of Death novels, films, paintings, television shows and computer games.

But here Dance of Death refers to the interactive posturing of two groups as they prepare for war.

Leslie—Why did the lecturer say preparation for war was like a courtship?

Irene—Because the communities about to go to war were like addicted lovers; they so focused on each other. Groups began taking the preparatory military steps to wage war on each other when the need for the human blood sacrificial ritual began rising in each society. There was increasing distain for more nuanced analysis; the political process consisted of focusing on injustices, amplifying the sense of righteousness and playing the blame game. Thinking became more and more simplified and the potential enemy was increasingly dehumanized.

Finally, for war to break out, the group needed to "come together" led by a charismatic leader, usually a father figure. As war began, irrational feelings took center stage. The depersonalization of the people on the enemy side had to be completed by then; this was a *sine qua non* to get the young soldiers to overcome their innate sense of empathy and to kill strangers.

Leslie—What do you mean by depersonalization?

Irene—As we know today, depersonalization is actually a mental illness—there is a psychiatric disease called the Depersonalization Disorder. These patients feel unreal themselves. Brain imaging techniques demonstrate abnormalities in both the sensory cortex and an area of the brain called Brodmann's area 7B that positively correlates with test scores of depersonalization and dissociation[1]. These are individuals who feel utterly depersonalized themselves.

However in primitive times, it was quite different; people didn't recognize their own thinking as depersonalized in wartime; rather, they thought of the enemy as depersonalized. At that time, depersonalizing of an enemy was an important part of constantly reinforced political propaganda in preparation for war. The enemy would be called degrading and inhuman names. It affected the thinking of virtually all members of the group.

Leslie—How could people be so affected by such group thinking?

Irene—Looking at it historically, the purpose of the Dance of Death actually became more and more disguised as the primitive period moved on, so what was going on was not immediately obvious to many. By the twentieth century, war propaganda was developed into a high art, beginning its work from the very start of each Dance of Death phase. First by jokes and then supposedly true horror stories, the population of the Dance of Death partner and its soldiers were gradually rendered as evil persons. Another example of depersonalizing people in preparation for death is how totalitarian regimes gradually would destroy their own leadership. An example of one of the most successful uses of propaganda ever devised were the polished lies of Lenin and Stalin of the Soviet Union. They were such brilliant propagandists that even "Stalin's terror arose with his victims' eerie compliance." [2]

Leslie—What about the members of a group who favored diplomacy and peace?

Irene—Once prewar preparations have begun, it was very difficult to stop the inevitable. But since war was preplanned and took time to get going, there would appear to be the possibility that diplomacy might stop a war. This then raised the question that the primitives pondered—if a war occurs, is it because of the failure of diplomatic negotiations? In other words, in such situations do wars occur by default rather than by design?

Leslie—Give me an example.

Irene—Take what happened in Britain before World War II as an example of trying to stop war by diplomacy. Politically both the left and the right in England were rethinking war after the horrible trench warfare slaughter of World War I; apparently the human blood sacrifice ritual was overdone. It exceeded the sacrificial quotient[3] that was necessary to satisfy the group's need for blood-letting of its own members.

On the left, strong antiwar feeling and pacifism developed. Less noted were the developments on the right; Lloyd George's private secretary Philip Kerr felt personally guilty because he had written the notorious "war guilt" clause into the Treaty of Versailles. This clause incorrectly stated that World War I had been caused solely by German aggression, deeply offending the Germans. It has been argued that his own guilt may have been a factor in the involvement of Kerr along with many other conservatives in the diplomatic appeasement movement toward Nazi Germany during the 1930s. But this appeasement of Hitler by the British as well as diplomatic maneuvers by other countries was really just part of the Dance of Death toward World War II in Europe at that time. [4]

Leslie—So are you saying that guilt underlies appeasement?

Irene—Wishing to avoid group murder is a healthy, good thing! As you shall see in a later lecture, societies that tilt toward guilt are more likely to actually avoid war than societies that tilt toward shame. However in most situations in primitive history, war had its own ritualistic necessity and would not be denied. In such situations, diplomacy became part of the prelude, while the arms began to build up. The pressure would become overwhelming as the Dance of Death developed into a fatal waltz, as the armed men dancing with their opposites began to fill whole ballrooms. Then war would occur, by design.

Although we know that war met an underlying irrational need of the primitive groups, any number of apparently rational reasons for war would be discussed during the Dance of Death period. The next lecture is devoted to that topic.

CHAPTER 6

▼

THEORIES ABOUT THE CAUSES OF WAR

Abstract 1006 There were many, many excuses for mass murder in primitive times. Biological evolutionists accused our "animal nature", economists correlated economic downturns with war, political scientists referred to power, boundaries and forms of government, and the psychoanalysts attributed war to inborn aggression plus poor child-rearing practices by mothers.

Leslie—Well that was a pretty interesting lecture on the etiologies of war, the *casus belli*. The lecturer stressed that as the cultures became industrialized, they increasingly became civilizations of artifice, parody, even full masquerade. There was so much slanted information. Do you suppose that this triumph of propaganda became increasingly more effective in Dance of Death situations, leading up to a war?

Irene—It is likely. In those times, people who participated in a war often believed that a war began when their group experienced a surprise and unexpected attack. Sometimes the leadership would even stage a fake attack to start a war. However as the Dance of Death preparations for war were gradually better understood, it became undeniable that wars were planned for by both sides; there was more than one dancer. This led the thinkers of primitive times to try to understand the underlying causes of their wars.

Leslie—So what did they figure out?

Irene—There was no shortage of theories regarding the causation of war. Biological evolutionists accused our "animal nature", economists proposed that economic downturns caused war, political scientists referred to political power factors or geographical factors, and psychoanalysts attributed war to inborn aggression and/or poor child-rearing practices by mothers. It was understood that there may or may not have been some merit in each of these claims; certainly there can not be only a single isolated cause of such a complex behavior as war. In fact there were many, many excuses for mass murder in primitive times.

Leslie—What do you think about it?

Irene—I personally suspect that for such a horror as deliberate human blood sacrifice in the form of war to be consistently seen in virtually all human communities from the cannibals to the early postmodern globalized empires, there must have been a fundamental underlying human thread. Shall we review the theories from the lecture?

Leslie—I have to admit I thought that the idea that <u>the "animal" nature of humans</u> might have caused both individual violence and war seemed reasonable to me.

Irene—But as you heard, this is a calumny against animals. Very few animals ever kill their own kind.

Since the people from the primitive era loved to project their own murderous fantasies inappropriately on to animals [1], there was a lot of focus on the rare examples where animals actually do kill their own kind (acting like humans!). Animal infanticide is the main way that animals have of killing their own species;

examples have been documented of lions, wolves, hyenas, gorillas and chimpanzees killing infants of their own species in the wild. Caged, depressed animals were even more likely to kill their young.

Leslie—Do adult animals of the same species kill each other?

Irene—In the case of individual adult *versus* adult violence, usually the closest it is ever seen in most <u>vertebrates</u> between adults of the same species is the struggle over mating between male animals. However even there, in the case of most vertebrates, the struggle usually ends not in the death of the loser, but rather in the loser making a stereotyped gesture of defeat. A somewhat similar pattern can be found among the <u>invertebrates</u>—the loser in an invertebrate mating struggle commonly gives a low-intensity version of a display shown at full intensity in courtship, which then tends to terminate the attack.

Leslie—Do animals ever conduct wars, one group against another?

Irene—Regarding the possibility of war, many animals like to mark their territorial areas but wolf packs do not conduct "war" against each other. In fact, there is almost no evidence of adults of the same species killing each other in any organized fashion. The chimpanzees—our nearest relatives in the animal world—were the closest to an animal example of group violence; it has been documented that occasionally a band of chimpanzees as a group might beat up individual members of another band, one by one. This animal "war" at best resembled a pathetic neighborhood gang fight among adolescents rather than anything resembling a human war [2].

Leslie—Yes, I've heard a lot about the chimpanzees.

Irene—According to de Waal, a primatologist who studied these animals, the twentieth century theoreticians might have had different ideas about the inevitability of violence in human society and about male dominance and bonding in hunting and warfare had the bonobo (pygmy chimpanzees) been known to scientists first and the regular chimpanzees second.[3] The differences between bonobos and chimpanzees were only slight in terms of the amount of aggression, but greater in terms of reconciliation afterwards. The bonobos were more socially cohesive and, under crowded conditions, they increased the amount of appeasement signals and grooming contact.

Actually one of the great surprises of studying chimpanzees was that these primates were demonstrated to have a culture, which was passed by learning through the generations, not just by their genes.

Leslie—This subject reminds me; have you heard the latest gossip—that the Institute of Ancient Primatology has begun the process of trying to reconstitute the extinct bonobo, that cousin of the chimpanzees. They are going to try to blend ancient DNA with a still living primate. Ever since bonobos became extinct back in primitive times, this has been on the agenda of the Institute.

Irene—But to the extent that chimpanzees and possibly bonobos had a culture, that can't be reconstituted by genes alone. You can't clone cultures with DNA. Genes and culture co-evolved.

Leslie—Anyway, I understand the basic point that chimpanzees didn't conduct war, but what about the armies of ants?

Irene—The primitives were fascinated by the world of ants and called some ants "army ants." It is true that ants appear to have some humanlike characteristics. The famous leaf-cutting ants, whose processions look like a multitude of animated leaves on the march, seem almost human because at home they are ant farmers who create gardens. Inside their nests, they cultivate and grow special kinds of mycelial fungus on a leaf mulch; the colony eats the fungus as their main source of food. But another famous type of ant, the so-called army ants, do not have armies in the sense that the leaf-cutters had gardens. Their "armies" are not like human armies. The purpose of these mass movements is strictly to obtain food; the ants are out to kill and slice up other insect species, not other ants, as a food source for the colony. Army ants are particularly fond of wasp larvae as well as katydids and grasshoppers. Furthermore these swarms or columns of ants are quite unlike human armies; they are leaderless—each individual in the column seems to possess the ability to strike off in its own direction. The overall organization appears to be achieved by information each ant gets from pheromones—sociochemicals. The field operations of these ant armies fit the principles of hydraulics more closely than they do those of military tactics [4].

Leslie—So we have to give up on "animal nature" as being responsible for wars?

Irene—The basic problem with the animal theories was that conducting a war required motivation, planning, self-regulation, and self-monitoring—all aspects of prefrontal executive cognition which is unique to the human brain. Instead of imagining our "animal" nature, it would have been more accurate for the primitives to label that rare animal who actually did kill one of its own kind as having a "human" nature.

Leslie—So if animals so rarely kill their own kind and instead overwhelmingly use their aggressive skills to kill other species, why did the primitive people focus on and publish each one of those rare exceptions that they could possibly find? And even if animals did kill their own kind, why would humans want to imitate animal behavior?

Irene—Humans don't imitate animal behavior. We feel remarkably superior to all animals, including mammals. It is true that the internal sanctions that govern our behavior—shame, guilt and loss of self-esteem—appear to have evolved out of some genes which set different behavioral paradigms in other mammals. Our inward feelings of guilt and shame eventually contributed toward outward human group activities, like religion and war.

Leslie—So, even though we are human animals, we didn't imitate other animals?

Irene—I guess you could say that because we have, of course, animal brains, and because like a number of other mammals we are very group-oriented, in that sense our war behavior had a tangent relationship to our being human animals. But the violence of humans planning in advance to hurt other humans, rather than prey, was not imitative of other animals.

Our ancestors also studied a number of other theories about the cause of wars, as the lecturer mentioned.

Leslie—Such as the theory that <u>economic downturns cause wars?</u>

Irene—Yes, there were a great many war theories that dealt with economic downturns or imbalances as a cause of war. In the twentieth century, there were a lot of theories that the way that wealth was configured in capitalism or communism caused wars; both kinds of societies were full of horrible examples of killings and wars. The creation of a middle class was supposed to stop wars but it didn't; the creation of a working class society was supposed to stop wars but it didn't.

Leslie—But didn't hard times economically sometimes occur right during the period just before wars started?

Irene—Yes; it was not that there wasn't data that economic downturns sometimes preceded wars during primitive times, and actually that wars often were a factor in spurring technological progress. But as we look back on it now, what a strange solution indeed in economic terms! War consisted of throwing away not just human lives but also major amount of treasure on arms and nonproductive work; both the victors and the vanquished suffered enormous economic losses, in spite of attempted reparations. War was the human activity least likely to produce economic benefit to a group as a whole, in spite of major war-profiteering by the elite.

The waging of a war deliberately destroyed carefully accumulated human wealth. *There obviously was some other factor than pure economics involved here.*

Leslie—So you are saying that poor economic times could lead to even more destruction of human wealth by war? It all sounds a bit on the irrational side; how could rational people destroy more wealth when they were most worried about it?

Irene—To approach it rationally will not explain the reality of what happened in the histories of wars. As we know from all sacrificial rituals, losing valuables is the essence of sacrifice. War certainly meets the criteria of economic sacrificial loss— a big sacrificial ritual not only wasting human lives but also wasting human wealth on both sides of the Dance of Death.

Leslie—How about the victors in wars, the empires, who seized control of groups of other people, economically valuable land, minerals, and other valuables from the losers?

Irene—Fighting over resources, such as oil in the twentieth century, undoubtedly was a consideration in a lot of human killing. These resources tended to benefit the selected few at the top of the hierarchy of the conquerors. It was a hierarchy issue; all things considered, the group as a whole definitely were losers. Like all sacrificial rituals, the strong killed the weak. Remember that war—the people killed and wounded, the money involved, the time and creativity diverted—was a gigantic project of wasting resources. But the leadership tended to dissemble on this issue, and was careful to put the call to war in political, rather than economic, terms.

Leslie—So what were those <u>political factors</u> that rallied whole groups of people to go to war? How about fighting about boundaries; wasn't that a political cause of war?

Irene—Political or geographical—certainly many scholars in primitive times believed that the desire for territorial gain or territorial conflict on a border incited wars. In 1975, a scholar developed the application of mathematics to international relations[5]. His detailed statistical analysis of all wars in the world from 1820 until 1947 revealed a geographical etiology of wars. His study found that states tended to become involved in wars in proportion to the number of other states with which they had a common frontier; however borders were mostly relevant in the smaller states. In those states, the study found that "contiguity has been an important factor in war" during the period where the statistics were collected.

Of course this finding was suggestive of the old *power and boundaries* issue. Geography may have been a factor, but there were plenty of borders between states where war never occurred at all. The Great Wall of China was designed with the concept that erecting barriers and being isolated would protect a society from wars, but we now know that isolation is not a harbinger of peace.

To many scholars of war, it was not a physical boundary but an intangible creed, an ideology, that was most responsible for the human blood sacrifice of wars. They singled out the special ideologies woven into the *identification politics* of tribalism or nationalism. Also accused of being responsible for war were other ideological-type identities such as those of an institutionalized religion or a secular religion such as communism.

Leslie—Why were people so influenced by ideologies?

Irene—I'm not sure, and it must be quite complicated, but I suspect that one underlying factor was that human beings of those primitive times were quite hungry for meaning to their lives. That hunger may have driven much of what they come to politically believe and act out. Ideologies with clear cut answers, even including those obviously leading to violence, cruelty and war, became very attractive to the meaning-hungry. Ideologies promising moral superiority in particular turned out to be almost irresistible in history of the primitives.

Leslie—But even in the same historical era, couldn't there be apparently quite different ideologies dominating different groups?

Irene—Well, we have to concede that since virtually all groups had wars in primitive times, they decided to go to war while coming from an immense variety of disparate, sometimes contradictory, ideologies. Developing a huge number of different ideologies is what humans do when seeking group solutions to the same or similar human problems. A brilliant thinker in primitive times, Mesulam, put it this way—actually, it is my favorite quote!

> In almost all other animals, genetic factors constrain behavioral domains such as those involved in dietary preferences, methods of communication, courting displays and affiliative interactions. The situation is drastically different in humans, where thousands of languages have been invented to express the same thoughts, thousands of cuisines to satisfy the same hunger, and thousands of diversions to dissipate the same boredom. An ability to tolerate and seek novelty underlies the unique human aptitude for discovering multiple solutions to similar problems, a faculty that greatly accelerates adaptation to rapidly changing circumstances. [6]

Leslie—And thousands of ideologies, too!

Irene—Yes.

Leslie—But didn't the specific ideology of giving power to the people by secret ballot voting, that is, the ideology of the democratic form of government, decrease the violence in such a society?

Irene—In the eighteenth to the twentieth century, intellectuals wondered if *the form of government itself* might be determinative of the propensity to violence and war. According to this doctrine, changing political power by voting rather than by military coups resulted in democracies, which then tended toward peace, while totalitarian governments tended toward war. There was a lot of hope placed in the rule of law based on written constitutions.

Unfortunately this theory relied on form, not substance. Constitutions were barely any check when the group was ready for a killing spree. In spite of its somewhat restraining effect, law itself was used to murder people throughout the primitive period. What became clear is that the adequacy of adult suffrage and the exercise of majority rule is only one side of a coin. In the coin of constitutional democracies, majority rule were the patina side; protected minority rights were the essential shiny other side.

As it turned out, decreased violence and war that were correlated with majority rule actually were much better correlated with minority rights—the toleration of ambiguous impurity in society with all that that implies. This included movements toward equal rights for women, ethnic minorities, dissenters, the handicapped and foreigners. The lecturer today mentioned what the daughter of a Jewish man fleeing the Nazis in 1940 wrote:

> 'My father went first from Austria to Italy. *And then he made the mistake of fleeing from a fascist country to a democracy*, that is, to France. The Italians were much less prone to interfere with Jewish refugees than the French were, and in fact one of his brothers survived in Italy … it was in France that my father was handed over to the Germans.' [7]

Leslie—The last part of the lecture was about twentieth century <u>psychoanalytic theories about wars</u>. Apparently in the early twentieth century, according to the lecturer, a theory of the unconscious roots of human behavior was developed which included concepts underlying wars. The theory of kill (aggression) or die (death wish), as expressed by Sigmund Freud, resonated deeply with other intellectuals of that troubled time.

Irene—But by the end of the twentieth century, many of his ideas were challenged and often debunked[8]. Some of his ideas about human behavior were revealing, others too idiosyncratic. One of his most interesting concepts was applying selected principles of individual behavior to group behavior; this created the field of psychohistory which he founded. [9,10]

Leslie—How long did Freud's theories last?

Irene—From our vantage point looking back hundreds of years beyond the twentieth century, we can see that Freud was an early thinker in identifying the unconscious and its power, which we now study neurologically. Freud was most illuminating in his description of many of the mental mechanisms, which have stood the test of time. But the problem was that he himself and his followers also stumbled a lot; they were all part of a culture based on adult male fantasies, which included putting down women and children. Some of the group behavior theories regarding war were contaminated by fantasies about young men or about mothers.

Leslie—What's an example from Freud's theories of older men fantasizing about younger men?

Irene—There are a number of examples. One is the theory of the *primal horde*, where the dreaded primal father prevented his sons from satisfying their sexual impulses until they slew him transforming the paternal horde into a community of brothers. In real war situations, however, exactly the opposite happened; the leaders, the fathers, arrange for the killing of their sons, the soldiers.

Another example is the *Oedipal Complex;* a literature developed claiming that war could best be interpreted in oedipal terms [11]. The argument went as follows: the sexually-slowed down fathers arrange a premeditated mass murder of young sexually potent men, and these young men cooperate in their own attempted killing (war) because they were guilt-ridden by their unconscious oedipal drives to compete with and even replace their fathers. A more relevant borrowing from that Greek Oedipus story would have been the part where the father Laius attempts to kill his son Oedipus, because that better accords with what actually happened during wars—where the older men (fathers) sent the very young men (sons) out to be murdered.

In fact, this oedipal concept of psychoanalysis was the opposite of most real life families, where the ambivalent adult fathers, however much they loved their sons, could be jealous of the youth and health of these boys, to say nothing of the maternal love being bestowed on the boys by their wives. The psychoanalysts often described the sons as more hostile to the fathers rather than the other way around; the actual reality of the older men's feelings about the younger men was acted out in war scenarios which occurred at regular intervals.

Leslie—You said that in that primitive period the culture was putting down women, too? But I want to say, before you answer, that you are a fine one to complain about adult male fantasies; as a pretty woman, you had a great deal of advantage from them.

Irene—(Smiling) Both genders enjoy many of the adult male fantasies, but to judge from the psychoanalytic literature of the twentieth century, mothers were often denigrated. This is shown by some war theories from psychoanalysis blaming child-rearing practices of the mother as responsible for war. A book called The Psychoanalysis of War summed up the "curative" power of war regarding "psychotic anxieties" left over from bad childhoods [12]. It was an example of blaming women for how men were behaving.

Leslie—Didn't war have some "curative" powers?

Irene—Reviewing the history of wars during primitive times from the point of view of today, one can see that the psychoanalysts were not totally wrong when they referred to a therapeutic aspect of war. But their focused attacks on mothers (women) [13] obscured the actual function of wars, which were related to the whole group, both men and women, and the need for ritual sacrifice. That's tomorrow's lecture.

CHAPTER 7

▼

SACRIFICIAL RITUALS

Abstract 1007 Sacrifice describes a ritual in which something of value is given for a less tangible or ambiguous reward. Human blood sacrifice refers to public killing on behalf of the group, both for regular, planned rituals and also in times of crisis. What is sacrificed can be of value to others or it can be just wasted. The first human blood sacrifices may have been cannibalism, turning people into edibles; later they were seen primarily in wasting people, such as in wars, and its accompanying genocides. Human blood sacrifice is troubling to all concerned; sacrificial blood-letting has the psychological duality of both cleansing and staining.

Leslie—Well I finally got to understand something about history of wars—the lecturer stated plainly that she thinks that wars are *sacrificial rituals*. The way that these rituals are set up is by the underlying political excuse that future bliss justifies present sacrifice.

Help me go back to the most elementary of definitions—exactly what is a sacrifice?

Irene—To answer that question, I'll start with how sacrifice was defined in primitive times. But in truth, the underlying meaning of the word is not that different than it is today. The word "sacrifice" describes a ritual where a person or a group gives up or wastes something of value that is tangible or precious—for the purpose of obtaining a reward that is less tangible or even psychologically ambiguous. What is given up can be 1) useful to other people or 2) can just be wasted. In primitive times, sacrifices were mostly of the wasted, loss type. They could either be the destruction of things of economic or emotional value, or they could be the planned shedding of blood—wasting people. The goal of these sacrificial acts was to obtain a reward which could best be described as magical or psychological. Violence is often said to be "redemptive", another way of expressing the sacrificial nature of killing.

Leslie—When did humans become interested in sacrifices?

Irene—It is something very universal with *homo sapiens*. Sacrifice began to be described as soon as writing was begun, and it can be argued that there is evidence of sacrifice before written records. The Sumerians, who invented early cuneiform writing sometime just before 3400 BC, described sacrifice in detail, including the fact that one sacrifices the very best. The Gudea, cyl. A XVIII 7 reads "he sacrificed perfect oxen and perfect goats".[1]

In the earliest writing in China, the oracle bones of the Shang dynasty (c.1766-c.1027 BC), the character *ti* initially appears to have meant a sacrifice. Later the word *ti* was subsumed into the names of the divine ancestors for whom sacrifice was made. Humans are bargainers, including obtaining magical rewards.

<u>Human blood sacrifice</u> was the name that was used to describe the activity of groups of ancient people who had decided together to kill one or more human beings of their own group. Even if it was just one victim, this was not just another individual murder. It was a planned community activity, actually a deeply meaningful religious/political activity. In the English language, the word "sacrifice" was closely related to the word "sacred." This was a group ritual.

Leslie—When do rituals become sacrificial rituals?

Irene—Of course it is natural for human beings to have rituals—patterns of working, eating, sleeping, and relaxing that are comfortable. Rituals are useful; they allow the brain to reserve its analytic function for new events while ritualistic activities become automatic; rituals and rites are part of the lives of both individuals and groups of people. As parents know, some conscious ritualization of life-styles, with defined boundaries of behavior and activities, can be of great value to help children mature as they grow up.

When do rituals become sacrificial rituals? When there is a planned loss from a person that either goes into a wasted negative purpose or a positive purpose that helps someone else. But whether they are classified as wasting or helpful, negative or positive, sacrifices lead to a sense of satisfaction. In the case of individuals, small personal sacrifices can be built into lifestyles; they are found in all types of societies. The giving up of a bit of wealth on a regular basis, called tithing, to a church or a good cause were classic examples of individual sacrifice in the primitive period. Altruism is so emotionally satisfying because it contains the element of sacrifice; remember sacrifices lead to psychological rewards.

Leslie—But you were talking about sacrifices of the group, not the individuals.

Irene—Groups, such as states, also have a regular pattern (the group's lifestyle) of sacrifices. As with many individuals, such sacrificial activity of communities invariably involves a recurring wasting of wealth or giving it away at regular intervals; this is true in all groups studied up to the present time and probably is an unchangeable given of human group activity.

Unfortunately, in an overwhelming majority of these groups during primitive times, negative sacrifices predominated. The wasting of human life was included along with the wasting of treasure in the sacrificial practices recorded in the primitive histories. During those times, the sacrificial victim tended to be chosen both at the predestined times of ritual and also as the need arose. For example, the ancient Incas ritually sacrificed children at planned solstice ceremonies, but also sporadically in cases of drought, plague, earthquakes, famine, hailstorms, lightening storms, avalanches, when the Inca Emperor died, and in association with war and military victories or defeats.[2]

Leslie—But as societies advanced, didn't human sacrifice cease?

Irene—The answer is "No". Later in primitive times, this sacrificial wasting of human life by the group continued to be done under a more disguised form, yet in public under the aegis of law. Examples were capital punishment of a murderer; the death of the mentally ill (deliberately in Nazi Germany or by wandering homeless in other industrial societies) or the deliberate exposure of one's own soldiers to hostile fire. In the end, it all added up to the same thing—the group as a whole made decisions that resulted in the death of its own members.

Perhaps the best way to describe human sacrifice by twentieth century communities is "getting away with murder." It was obviously something very basic and essential since regular episodes of human sacrifice by groups are such a constant throughout primitive history. When the community arranged for the killing of a person in the name of the group's sacrificial goal, the blood was spilled without fear of reprisal; the death did not automatically entail an act of vengeance. Although the family of the individual victim mourned, the group as a whole got all the magic of blood-letting without paying an apparent price.

Leslie—What is that magic of blood-letting? What was the important psychological reward that the sacrificial ritual of murder brought to societies during primitive times? I am really interested in how they chose who was going to be killed. It is hard for me to fathom all this human sacrifice, particularly as late as the twentieth century.

Irene—Alright, we can go over the details of the lecture. First, the patterns of WHEN human blood sacrifice occurred, then WHERE it happened and WHY. If we can begin to understand that much, then perhaps the choice of victims— the WHO of human blood sacrifice—might become clearer.

Leslie—I do want to understand.

Irene—We'll start with <u>WHEN?</u> The history of the primitives suggests over and over again that human blood sacrifice was not only a timed ritual, but also appeared to be related to changes. The change might have been externally induced or self-induced. We all know for sure that incipient changes and the loss of routine are inevitable in this ever-changing world, and that the coming of changes can evoke much anxiety in human groups. All kinds of sacrifices, not just sacrifices of living things such as people or animals, tended to be conducted at the beginning of new events. Archeologists are always finding foundation sacrifices in the base of buildings, placed there as they began to be built. The beginning of a new agricultural cycle evoked a sacrificial ritual in many societies. A time of major political change or economic change would tend to evoke a sacrificial rite.

During primitive times, many forms of sacrificial activity were considered as an appeasement to the gods. Sacrifice was a technique used by the primitives at times of a change or crisis, likely based on the underlying assumption that the gods are all-powerful and control human events. Human progress, human creation of new things such as buildings, might have been worrisome because it was considered appropriating the creative power of the gods themselves. The group fantasy then followed that a sacrifice—the giving up of real, valuable things—would placate the gods at such moments of group hubris and avert the gods' jealousy. Sacrifice was also used as a belated token of gratitude when change had happened in a good direction—at celebrations to thank the gods when they were thought to have averted a disaster. Of course sacrifice to imaginary creatures, such as gods, meant wasting the resources in terms of the human population, thus classifying them as negative sacrifices (unless the priests ate the sacrificed animals after everyone went home).

Leslie—So you are saying that primitive groups chose the timing of sacrifices based both on 1) regular schedules, and 2) crises?

Irene—Yes. In the twentieth-first century, social science was very interested in quantifying ideas, so the concept of *the sacrificial quotient* was developed. It was developed as an attempt to create a numerical system of figuring out when the next war would occur or when the group could no longer tolerate a war. The observation had been made that a very long war with many sacrificial victims tended to delay the start of the next war, while a short war had the opposite effect, bringing the next war sooner.

Leslie—So exactly how was *the sacrificial quotient* calculated?

Irene—It is based on the collective shame/guilt variable, which is different in each society.[3] In a prewar situation, it is:

time since the last war X collective guilt/shame variable = sacrificial quotient

Leslie—I guess I could imagine how it possibly might be relevant in countries cycling through war, for trying to calculate when a war was going to end or when the next war might start. So the *sacrificial quotient* helped anticipate when the Dance of Death was about to begin?

Irene—Theoretically. The collective shame/guilt variable was different in each society and gradually changed over generations. Each group of people had their own specific history, their own foreign relations, their own contemporary zeitgeist, their own complex factors determining the collective shame/guilt variable for them as a nation.

Leslie—And the sacrificial quotient was useful in helping to predict when a war would end?

Irene—Yes, when a war was underway, *the sacrificial quotient* was:

$$\frac{\text{number of deaths of their own people}}{\text{total population}} \times \text{collective shame/guilt variable} = \text{sacrificial quotient}$$

Leslie—How about the deaths of the enemy soldiers, the "body count"? The non-combatants killed on the other side? Didn't they figure in the quotient?

Irene—Unfortunately, it rarely made any difference at all during primitive times. In spite of the boasting of the military, it could be 1 enemy dead or 1000 dead; it wouldn't make any difference in the end. To each side of the conflict, war was actually a sacrificial event of their group only, an acting out of group needs with its own specific deadly agenda.

Leslie—But there are so many factors other than war dead that determined when a war ends. Shouldn't they have been included in the *sacrificial quotient*?

Irene—There are many other realistic variables that modified each war situation in history. The sacrificial quotient measured the non-acknowledged, magical, group-psychological factors that got the war started in the first place and determined how soon it ended. War was a sacrificial event.

Leslie—But, if as you say, all states have regular sacrificial patterns, what about the few groups which had abjured war?

Irene—In societies which rejected war, the *sacrificial quotient* could still be of use, but was even more complicated to determine. The calculation of non-bloody sacrifices could have been used to anticipate possible trends in politics—more wasted sacrifices; swing to the right; more altruistic sacrifices, swing to the left. We know that these warless societies had heavy schedules of public sacrificial rituals.

Leslie—And you say these were public, that is, political/economic/religious enactments of sacrifice? This raises the question of <u>WHERE</u> did the sacrificial acts take place.

Irene—The important thing to know about where the sacrifices occurred is that they were not hidden, secret events. No, to be psychologically efficacious for the community, to relieve the community of its bad feelings, the sacrifice had to be a shared public event. The community gathered around to observe the sacrificial deaths—from cannibal tribes to the French Revolution, the killing was on public display for all to see.

Leslie—But the killing wasn't always in public?

Irene—You're right; later on, as the population grew and possibility of direct witnesses lessened, the media became the public forum. The chamber for capital punishments and the deaths of soldiers on the battlefield were less visible, but they were recorded and reported on in great detail by the media so all could know about them. That such killings by the group actually constituted a sacrificial rite became more and more disguised with time, as other reasons were given for them. But the slaughter itself still remained in the public arena for all to know about. The Where of a sacrifice was a public happening.

Leslie—It is time for <u>WHY?</u> This is what I am most curious about. Why on earth would groups of people need such public displays of human sacrifice? You hinted it was related to both rituals and crises, but I need a better answer than that. Did the people who committed these atrocities know why they were doing it?

Irene—According to the historical record, if one asked an executioner after it was all over, he replied "There is no reason *why* … They invented many reasons to kill people. They were all excuses and lies." [4]

Leslie—Killing for the sake of killing?! Who said that?

Irene—A killer in the Cambodian genocide who was responsible for 14,000 murders. But to answer your critical teleological question of why wars did occur, why there was so much human bloody sacrifice by groups during the primitive period is to get to the heart of the matter; this is a topic which still is relevant today.

To start with a historical example which shows that these practices were already underway as soon as writing was invented, the lecturer went back to the very earliest writing we know about; it was developed by the Sumerians of Mesopotamia about 3500-3400 BC. The first writing was pictographs (a type of picture) on clay tablets that were later developed into syllabic writing. Soon another group of people called the Akkadians who were living there with the Sumerians began to write their own language in Sumerian cuneiform. Dictionary-type clay tablets were prepared to translate the language of the one people into the language of the other.

When one looks at the cuneiform entry for "demon", the tablet said, first in Sumerian, "a god who has nobody to give offerings and decorations to his shrine". This is the equivalent in the Akkadian side of the dictionary to "an evil god/a demon." Thus this most ancient of tablets suggests that, in these old Mesopotamian cultures, regular offerings (sacrifices) to the gods were thought necessary to prevent gods from becoming evil demons and causing human misery. Another way to look at these entries is that humans have the power to prevent a god from becoming evil by attending to the god's needs at his shrine—by regularly giving up, sacrificing, things of human value to the imaginary deity. Here sacrifice clearly has an anticipatory, propitiatory function.

Later Theophrastus, (the ancient Greek philosopher who succeeded Aristotle as head of the peripatetic school), wrote that Phoenician and Greek sacrificial practices may have originally developed from cannibalism. He probably knew about the rituals performed at the sanctuary of Zeus atop Mount Lykaion by a people the ancient Greeks themselves described as "older than the moon." It was rumored that they performed a yearly murder, dismemberment, and communal eating of a child at the mountaintop. [5]

There is a book, Cannibalism: Human Aggression and the Cultural Form, which also describes cannibalism as the likely beginning of the practice of human sacrifice.[6] Since human beings are social creatures programmed to be empathetic to other humans, the cannibal feast likely was not an undiminished joy of eating, as it would have been with a slain nonhuman animal. The killing of a person in preparation for a cannibal feast undoubtedly included an ambivalence, perhaps even an element of trauma, just as all killing of humans does. The author noted that the group killing of a victim rapidly took on elements of magic and symbolism later exemplified by the practice of the head-hunters.

Leslie—Cannibals and head-hunters! What's next!

Irene—Calm down; you asked why there is human blood sacrifice and I am trying to answer. Historians believe that when agriculture and animal husbandry allowed relief from regular episodes of famine, groups may have abandoned cannibalism. Then the group murder (sacrifice of a human being) became ritualized, and was switched from hunger satiation to the magical and psychological realm. If one accepts that the concept of traumatic reliving occurs within groups [7], then reenactment of the earlier cannibal killings might be expected in later group customs in more covert and acceptable forms. In fact bits of symbolic cannibalism remained in the group culture in post-cannibal times, often separated out as the customs of children, possibly as a remembrance of the childhood of the group. Examples were the gingerbread men eaten at Christmas and the three-cornered pies of Haman's ear eaten on the Jewish holiday of Purim.

Leslie—So you are suggesting that it was the crime of cannibalism that led to human blood sacrifice?

Irene—To quote a psychologist of the later primitive times, who was writing after cannibalism had been eliminated by the effective control of famine:

> "A sacrifice combines both a reenactment of a crime which gives forbidden satisfaction and a punishment for the commission of this or a similar crime … If performing a sacrificial act is a reenactment of a crime, then we might suspect that in the case of human blood sacrifice the original crime might

have been murder. If the sacrifice entails destroying wealth or property, it might have been some form of theft, exploitation or coercion." [8]

Leslie—So once famine was eliminated, then did human blood sacrifice persist in a form other than overt cannibalism?

Irene—Definitely. During later primitive times, where we have extensive written records for information, each culture developed its own special rationale for sacrifice; there were many different forms of sacrifice and many different theories to rationalize them [6]. But underlying them all, there appeared to be the repetitive agenda to obtain relief from bad feelings of the group. Actions that had once been triggered by hunger for food in the group may have evolved into actions that gave relief from any number of shared group anxieties and bad feelings. These could be group feelings of powerlessness or impotence in the face of threats, anxiety about important changes or scary feelings of group incompleteness or emptiness. Particularly difficult were the deep feelings that the group contained members with sinfulness which causes pollution and contamination leading to danger for the group. If you look carefully at the artifacts, one can find just about any serious bad feeling!

Leslie—How about the reality that humans are animals themselves who are mortal and going to die. It seems to me that since human blood sacrifice is about death, it might have something to do with addressing the issue of human mortality. Since the group outlives the individual, could this be some kind of crazy, magical way of keeping the group alive and strong by an anticipatory killing of some of its weakest members?

Irene—Well, that anxiety about human mortality was one of many different concerns these sacrifices were meant to address. The reality is, of course, that human beings including their leaders are mortal animals, not immortal beings, with the inevitability of death and this was a theme that certain rituals tried to address. Real and then pretend sacrificial rituals became part of religious observances in primitive times, in part to address the specific human response to that unfortunate inevitability.

All living creatures, from ants to people, try to prevent or put off their own deaths by a variety of maneuvers. The brilliance of the human mind in primitive times was put to work devising innumerable solutions under the magical aegis of "life after death." The primitives went to great lengths to deny that human beings are animals as mortal as the other animals around them. Many of them simply couldn't accept that there is nothing more that each human can personally hope for than a healthy and long life that is telomere-programmed not to last.

Leslie—What is a telomere?

Irene—Telomeres are the ends of chromosomes that diminish with age and when they shorten too much, we die.

Leslie—So was human mortality the main anxiety leading to human sacrificial activity?

Irene—No, human mortality was only one of many concerns that appeared to underlie the purpose of those sacrificial rituals of groups of people, the human blood sacrifices, which were attempts to restore feelings of goodness, intactness, sanctity, purity as well as magic immortality. Whatever event had caused the bad feeling—that catastrophe, that misery, that pollution must be washed away. Found over and over again was the overwhelming need for pollution-removal, for moral superiority, which drove the sacrificial act.

Those standards that determined the feelings of goodness and moral superiority were based in most human societies during primitive times on religious precepts, often related by prophets who convey the opinions of the gods. The group turned to these gods—parental figures for adults—in times of crisis; they were the backup support system of each group when trouble loomed. Human blood sacrifice often appeared to be a group response to lack of control of a situation. The assumption in the past appears to have been that, when humans have lost control, the all-powerful gods must have that control and must be magically placated. Since the human community often bequeathed infinite power to these gods and since the normal life of any human community is full of mishaps, the subject of appeasement of the gods (sacrifices) came up sooner or later.

Leslie—How could sacrificing a person appease a god?

Irene—There is a possible overt motive for the bloody human sacrifices recorded in the Hebrew bible; it might have been the magical thinking that a killed person goes up to the heavens and could be an ambassador who could intercede for the group with the gods at closer quarters than any mortal being back on earth could [9]. On another continent, the Incas did wish their child sacrificial victims to be attractive and to "die happily" because they were the Incas ultimate messenger service, the *chasqui*, to the gods [2].

Leslie—Wasn't sacrificing children eventually replaced by sacrificing animals?

Irene—Not fully replaced; only partially replaced. However with time, people became more and more uneasy about their need for human blood sacrifice. There were numerous attempts to move beyond it. The ancient Greeks addressed the issue of human sacrifice in their morality plays. The story of King Agamemnon tells of how he sacrificed his daughter instead of an animal so his ships could sail to Troy; in the end he must die for it and is killed by the child's mother, his own wife. The Hebrew bible also had the story of a sacrificial substitution—the story of Abraham and Isaac—this time the animal is sacrificed instead of the child; the animal becomes a scapegoat [10]. It has even been suggested that another symbolic substitute for child sacrifice in that ancient society was the circumcision of male infants [8]. Animal sacrifices also occurred to celebrate when good things happened—such as thanking the gods for saving the group or its leader from harm. 100 cows and 200 lambs were sacrificed in Afghanistan to express gratitude when their new leader, Hamid Karzai, escaped assassination [11].

Leslie—So sacrificing animals worked and stopped human blood sacrifice?

Irene—The evidence suggests that the attempt to truly move beyond bloody human sacrifice was usually not successful during primitive times. Human sacrifice continued, but its purpose became increasingly disguised. Killing of people by the group, by the state, continued but with a degree of deliberate misunderstanding, a partial concealment of the reason for the killing—but never complete denial or else the rite of sacrifice would have lost its potency and efficacy. The twentieth century, for example, was truly an overload of public horrors of wars and murders. During that century, a reformer and peace activist named Martin Luther King understood his role to be like that of a modern sacrificed Christ; he said: "I shall chose my own Golgotha." He was assassinated.

Leslie—What was Golgotha?

Irene—The place where Christ was killed.

Leslie—It's amazing how long Christianity lasted; for more than two millennia. Do you know why?

Irene—Like Buddhism, there were many reasons, but an important one that many authors have noted was that the great success of Christianity may be related, at least in part, to the successful ritualization of a blood sacrifice. The son Jesus Christ appeased his father in heaven by his own sacrificial death. The symbolic re-enactment of his sacrifice inside the Mass generated purity (forgiveness of sins) by allowing those seeking holiness to symbolically re-experience the sacrificial death to the point of actually eating his divine flesh (the blessed wafer) and drinking his divine blood (the blessed red wine). This ritual comforted millions throughout primitive times.

Christ specifically said that his death was an atonement for the sins of all the people in the community—in other words, that it removed pollution from the group and restored purity to the group. This was a further development of a concept present earlier in Near Eastern culture when the killing of a single god restored the holiness of the remainder of the gods. A text from an ancient Mesopotamian Atram-hasis flood story (written more than 1000 years before Christ) said:

> *Let one god be slaughtered*
> *And the gods be thereby cleansed* [12]

In this very ancient story, even the gods themselves need cleansing; and the gods designate one of their divine members to be the sacrificial victim that removes pollution. Blood-letting washes away that moral impurity. It is the ultimate psychological cleanser.

Leslie—Why is blood-letting such a psychological cleanser?

Irene—It is hideously interesting. How violence purifies, how the shedding of blood is a purifying act, is a concept much explored in primitive times. Blood is the essence of life itself so how did the letting of blood purify? Apparently it has been imagined that human blood can be "polluted" by the thoughts and actions of its owner. Bad thoughts, bad blood; bad actions, really bad blood. Even doctors used a crazy theory of imbalanced (i.e.bad) "humors" in the blood from ancient Greece until well into the eighteenth century. This supposedly therapeutic medical bleeding often was disastrous for the patient, but no one seriously challenged it for two millennia. All that inappropriate medical blood-letting was suggestive of psychologically "polluted" blood being purified.

Leslie—Why was a *blood bath* synonymous with a massacre? Who gets the "bath" in a blood bath?

Irene—This is another example of blood-letting washing away pollution. It was the killer group that imbibed and reestablished its magical purity from the blood of those who were sacrificed; the murderers themselves were the ones who got the cleansing "bath."

Leslie—So blood-letting is magical cleansing?

Irene—Apparently, it seems that the ritual of human sacrifice (the blood-letting) was used during primitive times to achieve and maintain the necessary magic purification for a group. Throughout much of primitive history, a religiously pure group was thought by its members to be the ultimate form of a superior group. It was a top priority for most groups to always stay morally superior and as pure as possible. When such a group had a serious setback, the group superiority/ purity could be reestablished by its ability to wash away its impurities by using the purifying blood of other less powerful members of its own society. All human sacrifice had that element of magic cleansing. In the case of the genocides, to spill the contaminated blood of European Jews (Nazi Germany) [13], adults who speak French (the Khmer Rouge of Cambodia) or Tutsi women who were "lascivious seducers" (the Hutu-dominated Rwandan government) magically helped cleanse the killer group of its impurities.

And in order to be sure to get the magical credit, the group carefully, obsessively, kept a record, just as many individual serial murderers do. This explains the apparently baffling finding of careful and detailed records kept by the Nazis of the Jews killed in the extermination camps [14], the records complete with photographs found in the murdering prisons of Saddam Hussein [15], the detailed records of killings with photographs found even in the killing centers with limited resources, such as those of the Khmer Rouge of Cambodia [4]. The murderers did not maintain those records to help family members in the future find out what happened to their relatives. Those records were being carefully kept as an essential proof of the sacrifice, as a documentation of magical cleansing acts.

Leslie—This is horrifying and confusing. This lecture was primarily about blood as purifying, yet I had always thought that spilling blood resulted in more violence. Once violence started up, wasn't there more violence of the revenge type?

Irene—Yes, you are right; that is an important piece of the puzzle. There is no question that blood-letting has a duality. It had the capacity both to cleanse and but also to stain, both to purify but also to contaminate. Spilled blood could appease anger, but also drive men to more violence. It all depended on whose blood was spilled. This is the upcoming lecture about the <u>WHO?</u> of human blood sacrifices in primitive times.

CHAPTER 8

▼

THE BLOOD OF THE BELOVED

Abstract 1008 How were victims chosen when a group prepared to perform a human blood sacrifice? They could be identified by the Double Identity Rule—a true sacrificial victim must represent the group, must be a member of the group (identity one) yet have a characteristic which sets him apart from the whole group (identity two). Soldiers were members of the group, yet in a particular age group, also usually males. They were an example of group members sent on missions on behalf of the group where they could potentially die, and then the group would publicly mourn them—these were the criteria of human blood sacrifice.

Leslie—What a lecture about WHO was chosen to be the victims of human sacrifice! I really find it hard to believe when it comes to the very large numbers and types of people chosen during primitive times. Are you sure that the lecturer was not exaggerating?

Irene—Apparently the drive for human blood sacrifice by groups was so powerful in primitive times that one can make the argument that victims could be chosen for almost any reason at all, even opposite reasons in different societies. The Incas killed selected children because they were beautiful (suitable to meet the gods) while the Nazis selected out their own German criminals to be killed just because they were ugly.[1]

Leslie—The lecturer started out by discussing the form of human blood sacrifice of one or just a few individuals on behalf of the group, as practiced in early primitive societies and then later on in capital punishment.

Irene—This was a ritual where both the executioner and the victim had a special status within the group. In the case of the executioner, he often took on a semisacred role since he was performing a magical/religious act for the group. One thoughtful writer called him the "sacred executioner". [2]

However, sometimes the executioner may have been partially tabooed by his uneasy society after the killings were over, and the felt need for sacrifice had passed. Virtually all the executioners were male. In the United States in the twentieth century, the executioner who killed the prisoners on death row was reported to be a job in great demand (!) and furthermore he was virtually indistinguishable psychologically from the murderers condemned to capital punishment. As one author, who examined some of these men psychologically, put it "his serial executions were but the latest manifestation of his paranoid rage." [3]

Leslie—But the victims in earlier historical periods weren't murderers.

Irene—No, they were usually children or other powerless members of a group. Many psychologists in the twentieth century believed that the sacrificial victims were selected out to represent the "bad" parts of ourselves and that killing the victims cleansed the group. Since the one main purpose of sacrifice appears to be the restoration of purity, I guess that this makes sense—that is, crazy sense. For example, the Nazis' desperate attempt to "purify" the blood of the German people was an acting-out of their own feelings of dirtiness and fatal contamination—the imaginary psychophysical illness that simultaneously affected both the body and spirit of the German Volk. [4]

The openly selected victims to be publicly murdered of the earlier primitive period were to some extent replaced by sacrificial substitutes, masking tricks and distancing events. But in truth there was no abatement of the ritual of human sacrifice with time; these remained group events which just appeared in a different public form as time went on. In the case of the genocides in the bloody twentieth/twenty-first centuries, there was barely an attempt to disguise what was happening—except, of course, as necessary to deceive the victims themselves.

Leslie—So how were victims selected by the group to be murdered?

Irene—The lecturer pointed to the consistent characteristic of the victims of human blood sacrifice, which historians call the Double Identity Rule. Concepts of identity are so fundamental that they underlie how we perceive ourselves and much of politics. A "double identity" was a neurotic distancing device for individuals, where they could shed off things they had done that they weren't proud of. The double identity gimmick was used to hate your other self, your double—that is, the hateful part of oneself projected outward to an imaginary other, who was really part of you. In the same way, it is possible that groups that were feeling badly about their group identity, and concerned that it may have been diminished or devalued by other groups, may have searched among their own membership for potential "doubles" on whom to pour their group distress. Consciously the double was "the other", but unconsciously it was also "the self."

The Double Identity Rule states that the human blood sacrifice victims selected must be members of the group, no matter how tangential, in order to be adequate sacrificial substitutes for the group itself. To cleanse and purify the group, to abolish pollution in the group, the sacrificial victim must stand in, must be a sacrificial substitute for that group. In fact historically, the potential victims often were so identical-looking to other members of the group that they had to be identified artificially. In one example, yellow was a color-coding often chosen to identify the potential victims: the yellow star was selected for the Jews in Germany during Nazi times, and the Sikhs and Hindus living in predominantly Moslem Afghanistan were forced by the Taliban to wear yellow clothes and fly yellow flags over their homes.

Leslie—So exactly what were the criteria that made a person a double identity target?

Irene—That the victim must somehow be eligible as a member of the group was a most important starting criteria; he must be a true sacrificial substitute. Minorities living inside the territory of the majority group were favorite victims in primitive times; the more integrated the minority was with the majority, the more eligible they became as ritual sacrifice victims. A true sacrificial victim must represent the group; he can not be completely outside the group or his death will not benefit his killers. Thus the victim must be associated with the group (identity one) yet somehow have a characteristic which sets him apart (identity two); these are the two "double identities" of the victims. A classic example of the projected self-hatred involved in double identity murders was the Khmer Rouge targeting of all French-educated Cambodians, even though (or because) the Khmer Rouge leadership picked up their extreme ideology which led to the genocide from French members of the Communist Party when they themselves were studying in France.

Leslie—You have mentioned how Khmer Rouge genocide selected some of their targets; how about the Nazi genocide?

Irene—The Holocaust of the twentieth century was the product of Germany—where the Jews were much better integrated into the society than in the Eastern European countries; many German Jews before World War II considered themselves more German than Jewish. The Jews of Germany met the double identity criterion because, as a group, they had become quite integrated into German society; they were of it. It is interesting that the theme of double identity was a part of German culture as expressed by the word *Doppelgänger*—the double of a man. The fantasy was that the *Doppelgänger* walked in the man's place or even might try to take his place. There were a number of ways in which the Germans and Jews of the Nazi period in Germany shared habits and fantasies that were called "a family resemblance." These shared traits included industry with obsessiveness, perseverance, thrift, frugality, strong religious sense, family values, respect for the written word and pretensions regarding absolutes and the secrets of the universe [5]. It also was noted that the Yiddish language, mostly a blend of Hebrew and Germanic dialects from around 1000 AD, sounded archaic and yet strangely familiar. This possibly may have made the Yiddish-speaking Jews appear to German speakers as eternal ghosts of the German past [6].

Leslie—Alright; in the case of the Nazis, I can see how the double identity definition might apply to the Jews, as well as the mentally retarded Germans, the gay Germans, the anti-Nazi Germans, and the many other Germans who were deliberately exterminated by the Nazis. But the Nazis also committed a Gypsy Holocaust or Porajmos, the "devouring". How does double identity apply to a group like the Gypsies?

Irene—It is puzzling why the Nazis set out to exterminate the Gypsies. The sadistic Nazis sent them off to concentration camps, where they had numbers tattooed on their arms, were used for medical experiments, gassed in the gas chambers in groups—in other words treated in a way indistinguishable from Jewish victims. However unlike the German or Jewish victims, the Gypsies—the Roma, Sinti and Jenisch—clearly were outsiders. They were without German identification except for a tiny minority who received German or Swiss citizenship. Most lacked identification because they continued to travel in spite of efforts, starting before the Nazi period, to force them into a sedentary lifestyle. (A very few intermarried Gypsies who did become sedentary actually served in the German armed forces during World War II.) But the overwhelming majority of Gypsies continued their itinerant life and ended up being selected for extermination camps. For these wandering Gypsies the question arises, how could they have served any sacrificial purpose for the German nation?

There is a startling answer to this major challenge to the Double Identity Rule. There had been a seventeeth century scholarly thesis which claimed that "the very first Gypsies were Jews who stemmed from Germany".[7] So psychologically the ground was set for a Gypsy double identity of being "secret Jews". However the Nazis were not fully confident that the Gypsies were Jews, so the Third Reich wasted a lot of precious manpower and money during World War II to study this issue. Two different agencies were engaged in research on the subject: the *Reichszentrale zur bekämpfung des Zigeunerwesens* and *Rassenhygienische Forschungsstelle*.[1] Gypsies were measured, examined physically, and family histories were taken by the Nazis.

By now I assume that you have come to expect combatants in war to waste resources for group psychological craziness. The apparently senseless pursuit of this "scientific" conclusion that Gypsies were Jews may well have been driven by a need to rationalize the Gypsy extermination inside Nazi racist ideology. Apparently these research institutes had the job of upgrading the Gypsies into legitimate sacrificial victims, just as the Jews were. That is, the Gypsies had to become part of the German nation in some tangential way and, since this clearly wasn't so, their status had to be changed to a group—the Jews—who had in large part successfully integrated into Germany well enough to serve as sacrificial victims.

Leslie—Are you saying that the Nazis themselves felt a strong need to remold the Gypsy identity, so that they were somehow part of the extended German group?

Irene—Yes, that is what the concentration camp records suggest. The behavior in the concentration camps toward the Gypsies—for example the "scientific" experiments on them there and the detailed record-keeping about them—suggests there was more to it than simply ridding Europe of an undesirable group.

Leslie—Much of this material is so extreme that it is hard to believe! Were crazy identity problems involved in the Rwandian genocide, too?

Irene—Hatred of one's double, one's *doppelgänger*—that is actually, of oneself—might have been a factor in the monstrous crimes that Pauline Nyiramasuhuko was alleged to have committed during the Rwandan genocide during the late twentieth century. The International Tribunal at Arusha indicted her with 11 charges, including genocide, crimes against humanity, and war crimes; she was the first woman to be charged with these crimes in an International Court.[8] Pauline was in fact part Tutsi and kept it secret as she rose in the ranks of the murderous Hutu government. Purging one's own "ethnic impurities", based on real or imagined ancestors, could have been a factor underlying particularly vicious behavior in any number of genocidal situations.

Leslie—So during the twentieth century were minorities in process of assimilation inside societies, particularly inside right-wing states, likely to be in great danger?

Irene—No, it wasn't the political structure of those states, or even fascism *per se* that led to such murderous behavior. A society had to be at a particular stage of extreme, troubled identity where it needed sacrificial victims, as Germany was in the 1930s. For example, during World War II, the Italian Jews would have continued to live mostly in peace with their neighbors, in spite of the fascist racial laws, if it had not been for the Germans. [7] Another example during that war period is the Jews who were assimilated in Bulgaria where, in spite of having a pro-fascist government, the community insisted on protecting them during World War II. The fact that a group within a society is assimilated and eligible for sacrifice did not mean it is in danger if that society itself is not in need of group sacrifice at that historical time.

Leslie—Here's a hard question—is it considered a double identity sacrifice if a community decided together to kill the very top members of a society, like the king or queen?

Irene—That is an interesting point. Actually a double identity victim, whose deliberate sacrificial death had a very major effect on a community, was that of the leader/king himself. His first identity was as a member of the group yet his second identity was separate, as the only king. Regicide has a powerful effect on society. The English poet John Milton wrote an historical defense of regicide (king-killing) to help the rebellious Puritans prepare for the royal sacrifice. [9] Some primitive historians gave a certain amount of credit for the development of advanced Enlightenment ideas to the aftermath of that killing of Charles I of England in 1649 AD, and for the spread of those ideas to the killing of Louis XVI of France in 1793 AD.

But, as a practical matter, it was easier to sacrifice the more powerless members of society, like young virginal girls or children. They have the double identity of being *bone fide* members of the group, yet not full adult members. Young children who have not yet reached puberty were apparently an especially attractive choice as victims perhaps because they are members of the group who also are nonsexual, i.e. may have more "purity" to magically impart to their killers. In primitive times, they were often chosen for the sacrificial rituals.

Leslie—But by the twentieth century, that was no longer going on?

Irene—(Sigh) Such child cruelty was not limited to early primitive times. During the murderous twentieth century, use of small children as active participants in war became more common. Among the most dreadful developments of the twentieth century was the creation of lightweight weaponry making it possible to use orphaned, kidnapped, or "family-volunteered" preteen children as frontline soldiers. In the Iran/Iraqi war of the 1980s, the ayatollahs of Iran recruited young children into the Basij militias as "Revolutionary Guards". These children were sent into Iraqi minefields to detonate the mines with their bodies; called the children of the keys, they had keys to the gate of paradise placed on chains around their necks. Another example was seen in the brutal long-term civil war in Sierra Leone at the end of the twentieth century where male children as young as 6 years of age were stolen from their villages to form the SBU—Small Boy Units—in the rebel army. Many were branded on their skin like cattle with the initials of the rebel army so they wouldn't run away from their new jobs of killing people.

Leslie—I am beginning to see why this lecture was titled The Blood of the Beloved.

Irene—That title referred to more than small children. It also referred to soldiers who usually were adolescents and younger adults. Unlike small children, it took cunning to get them to agree to enter into the situation of mortal danger to themselves. They would acquiesce due to appeals to the strong force of primary group identification, moral norms [10], patriotic propaganda, the combination of group and family coercion, combined with a resigned or even cheerful acceptance of such macho risks. Many of them felt the powerful human drive of social altruism to help their group. Like everyone else, they had very strong group identification.

Leslie—But, wait a minute! Isn't it true that the case of soldiers differed from more classic human sacrifice situation, because there the victim always died. We discussed before that in a battlefield, chance did play a role in who was killed.

Irene—True, most soldiers did not die after all; in fact, in order to carry on, many soldiers secretly adopted the defensive conviction that they were somehow unique and special and would not be the ones to die. However it was undeniable that soldiers on both sides of any battlefield were in fact victims; *they had been selected by their own group to be possible targets.*

Supposedly there was military training designed to diminish their chance of dying, yet its underlying purpose was to teach them to follow orders blindly, that is, to be ordered into life-threatening danger. Basic training was a special program designed to instill certain male values into weaklings just released from their "mother's form of coddling" as they grew up; it was to replace their sense of self derived from their family with a particular version of male attitudes. Basic training was designed to strip the soldier of his unique individuality and make him part of a ruthless hierarchy. In many ways the goal was to create a subordinate who immediately follows an order without a second thought. On the battlefield, these orders include going into an area of dangerous enemy fire where the young soldier might get horribly wounded or killed.

Leslie—Horribly wounded or killed?

Irene—Every soldier who entered a combat zone was taking a chance with his own precious life. When he died, it was truly <u>the blood of the beloved</u>. Soldiers exposed to enemy fire in primitive times were almost always the youngest members of adult society—the late teenagers or the young adults—and were usually male. In order to participate in this potentially suicidal activity, they had to have the element of ambiguity, of hope, of denial when they were under fire.

Leslie—Why do you call soldiers sacrificial victims, if most of them were going to survive?

Irene—What I want to stress to you, in order to understand what was going on, is that it is necessary to realize that outsiders simply could not have fulfilled the role of sacrificial victims. For example, the soldiers killed on the "other side" in a war did not meet this group need. Although this was not openly acknowledged, in the case of war the military and civilian victims on the other side didn't matter. Their suffering in the end was irrelevant, and they didn't count as a sacrificial offering on behalf of the group. In spite of the military bragging about body counts of the enemy as far back as 2400 B.C. (remember the first lecture?), the group as a whole had little interest in the deaths of the strangers on the other side.

Leslie—So each soldier that was killed could have been considered a sacrificial victim for the group, but not the soldiers or civilians killed on the other side?

Irene—I'll give you an example of this phenomenon when the United States fought with Vietnam in the twentieth century. The people in the United States knew exactly how many of their own soldiers died during the Vietnamese war— there was a Vietnam memorial with 58,235 names on it. But they had little idea indeed about how many died on the other side, which included Vietnamese and Cambodians.

Leslie—How many?

Irene—It is hard to be sure; there was one estimate of 2,000,000 people or more.

Leslie—So much death! So, if all this is true, how was it arranged to get their own soldiers to agree to be sacrificial victims? We were arguing about it after another lecture.

Irene—As you know, I believe that during primitive times a soldier who in war died as a human blood sacrifice for his group was the victim of a diabolical scheme. War was one of the cleverest inventions of ancient humankind when it came to meeting the needs of human sacrifice, and getting sacrificial victims to cooperate in their own deaths. It may have been the original and was certainly one of the most popular of the many disguised forms of human sacrifice. What happened was that two groups, both needing the sacrificial ritual at roughly the same time, entered into the Dance of Death. What were they up to? *They were arranging to have each other perform the job of the sacred executioner of their own insiders (their own young soldiers) chosen for human sacrifice.* Apparently in primitive times wars were a deliberate massive sacrifice of their own young.

Leslie—That's horrible; why didn't the parents of the young soldiers protect them?

Irene—I hate to tell you the answer to that. The question was—*who* sent the young soldiers out to the battlefield; *who* pronounced the possibility of a death sentence on members of a younger generation?

Leslie—Who?

Irene—The answer was—their own parents.

Leslie—Surely you must be kidding.

Irene—Unfortunately, no. The sanctimonius majority of each group, including their own parents, sent them. We have many recorded descriptions of wars during primitive times. In these wars, a series of older father figures—politicians, generals, admirals,—made military decisions that sent younger men to do the actual fighting and dying. The older father figure usually stood out of or back from the action and took little chance on getting killed himself.

It is also true, as far as we can determine, that the mothers almost always went along with the fathers during these primitive times. It may seem hard to imagine, but the mothers sometimes were even enthusiastic about the upcoming war, as they shared in the group fantasy. In spite of initial misgivings, the mothers concurred in letting their sons go off to both become trained killers and to be in a situation where they could be killed. The young soldiers perceived what was going on; among the many reasons that most did not resist being sent to war was to please their parents and their community. In other words, the young soldiers too shared in the group fantasy.

Leslie—What could possibly be serious enough to cause groups to need human blood sacrifice so badly that they arranged to put their own sons in such mortal danger?

Irene—The next lecture on purity and violence will explore some of those dark reasons.

CHAPTER 9

▼

PURITY AND VIOLENCE

Abstract 1009 Humans are social primates very aware of how others perceive them, wishing to be considered honorable and morally superior. An underlying concept of moral superiority is being unblemished or pure. Political groups also share their own specific concepts of group purity, which becomes more important when the group faces trouble. One of the politico-religious meanings of purity is homogeneity, that is, intolerance of people with other ethnic, religious or cultural backgrounds.

Individuals obsessing about purity often need rituals to help them; so do groups where such rituals often included violence and war. In the twentieth century, the ideologies that included major purification were very deadly. The goals of purifying class society (Marxists) and purifying bloodlines (Nazis) often resulted in horrifying rituals of violence and war.

Irene—Well, what did you think of that lecture? Did you know that moral judgments are often instant, and the mind is adept at coming up with plausible rationalizations for why it arrived at a moral decision, even if they were generated subconsciously? In ancient times, people belonging to a wide range of faiths, even atheists, tended to agree on more moral judgments than they disagreed about.

Leslie—Frankly, I found that part boring; I thought the section on utopias much more interesting.

Irene—Yes, it was surprising how many utopias there were in primitive history. The drive for *moral superiority* was the basis of a number of attempted utopias. In the search for either godly utopias or secular utopias, the common belief in perfect solutions was the most dangerous of political illusions! Sooner or later there was violence and war in an attempt to obtain that morally perfect utopia. The lecturer pointed out that in primitive times, even religions started by pacifists— Buddha, Christ—ended up with massive amounts of group murder in their name.

Leslie—So as people seeking utopias talked and tried to live by ideals which always included peace, what kind of collective mindset was undermining it, what brought about such sacrificial activities as war?

Irene—We know that all groups have shared bad feelings from time to time leading to a need to let off steam, but in the case of the utopias, the pressure was even greater. All communities can have anxiety about a lot of things including change and feelings of powerlessness. But, by trying to set up a utopia with moral superiority, there was the added fear of pollution from sins of members of the group. This often resulted in acquiescing to internal murder of their own ruling membership, as was seen, for example, in the supposedly-secular Stalinist Soviet Union and Cambodian Khmer Rouge.

Leslie—But most societies in the twentieth century and before that weren't trying to be utopias, yet they still had much violence and war.

Irene—Utopias are just an extreme example of what almost all countries engaged in—regular periodic wars, to the point that almost everyone that lived at those times actually thought that such wars were inevitable.

A case can be made that what all these communities were striving for by their violent sacrificial rituals was a healing good feeling to cleanse away their bad feelings as a group. Even though no state was a utopia, each society wanted to think of itself as *honorable, pure, and morally superior.*

Leslie—How do you know that?

Irene—You can see it most clearly in the historical Dance of Death artifacts. As a society moved toward war, the political climate became more and more focused on the absolutist goal of unquestionable moral superiority. Political nuances gradually would yield to a kind of black and white thinking. It could be called the necessity of *ingroup moral superiority thinking* prior to human sacrifice.

Leslie—But doesn't everyone want to be perceived as morally superior?

Irene—To be perceived by others as having high moral values—it didn't have to be reality, just perception (!)—is still one of the most precious human goals on the planet. This concern of so many individuals is an important cognitive template inserted into the groups that they belong to. Yet historically the unfortunate spin-off was that the societies most focused on moral superiority and purity were among some of the most destructively warlike on earth.

Of course to be concerned about being moral is to be human. We are social primates with an awareness of how others perceive us—even the mentally ill, the utterly narcissistic, the tyrannical criminal, the psychopath have a level of inner consciousness of shame, guilt and social norms which occasionally surfaces to everyone's surprise. Rare indeed was the individual criminal "monster" who had not done an occasional redeeming good deed in some other layer of his life, often for a family member.

And as it was with individuals, so it was with human groups. Some of the groups that had an intense rhetoric about moral superiority and purity were some of the most sadistic and murderous on earth. But even these extreme groups tended to retain some balancing activities; inside their own group, social good is balanced with their rigid obsessions with purity.

Leslie—Give me an example.

Irene—An example during the beginning of the twenty-first century was the difficulty in locating a terrible man, Osama Bin Laden, who developed guerilla war techniques specialized for killing large numbers of civilians; enormous resources were spent by his many enemies trying to find him. His Islamist followers however protected him due to a black and white "us vs. them" mentalities, where the pure "us" was perceived as magically good and holy compared to their impure nonIslamic opponents.

Leslie—I learned in history that in primitive times, many groups operating in poor communities, like the early Christians, altruistically helped the needy of their community in order to establish a religious ideology and build their base.

Irene—Although many started out very peaceful—Christianity was started by a leader who was actually a pacifist—sooner or later there was a swirling blend of violence stirred together with goodness on the people's plates. Particularly in the Western world, also in Japan, there were a number of subcultures, each from a religious base, which developed a focus on apocalyptic violence. In those groups, violence was conceived in sweeping terms as a purification and renewal of humankind through the total or near-total destruction of the planet. [1]

Leslie—What! How could that be? Why would a group get so focused on the need for purification that it could result in fantasies of destroying the planet?!

Irene—Cleanliness and purification are issues of both body and mind. People overly concerned with the issues of purity may have been trying to combat their own feelings of impurity that are natural to us all. It is no coincidence that major insults in all the primitive languages referred to the anal and genital parts of the body. However when becoming unduly focused on impurity, a self-destructive dualism of the pure and impure can develop, as occurred in apocalyptic groups.

Leslie—Well, everybody likes to be clean.

Irene—Of course. Feelings of contamination result in behavioral efforts to become clean; these "purifying" behaviors can be observed in both individuals and groups.

The concepts of purity/impurity have several layers of meaning. There is the first meaning of cleanliness and good sanitation to protect the individual human body. This is the physical meaning. A failure of purity or exposure to pollution can result in a susceptibility to disease that can be life-threatening. The concern with physical pollution can be a legitimate expression of an underlying fear of mortality. This reality may help account for the symbolic association of impurity with the darker forces of death.

A second meaning of purity is to lead a totally sinless life, a religiously pure life saints try to live.

We archival students of war are primarily concerned here with the third meaning—the politico-religious meaning of purity.

Leslie—I don't get it; what is wrong with wanting to be clean?

Irene—Usually nothing; it is a good healthy thing. How we think about being clean has been investigated; techniques for imaging the brain have disclosed that specific brain networks are involved in the concern about cleanliness.

However serious disturbance inside this brain circuit results in obsession about contamination and purity; such individuals can be diagnosed with a psychiatric disease called the obsessive-compulsive disorder (OCD). These individuals get stuck in repeating a once appropriate act, such as washing their hands after they touch dirt. But the act becomes inappropriate as they continue to wash their hands over and over long after the dirt is gone. They don't get the appropriate inhibitory feedback information inside their brains that the task is now completed; their anxiety about dirtiness is not relieved. These are compulsive acts based on intrusive thoughts and images; and these compulsive acts become quite inappropriate rituals for the individual. Sometimes the ritual occurs many times a day, and performing it helps relieve the patient's anxiety. It is interesting that patients with an early onset of such obsessive-compulsive behaviors sometimes may have at least one associated form of aggressive behavior [2].

In the past, many groups became overly concerned about contamination and purity in their societies, often in a cyclical fashion. This happened most often when the group deteriorated, with the members sharing anxiety or depression about an unfavorable political situation for their group. Increasing the group rituals in such a community was helpful in decreasing the general anxiety—just as it does for an OCD patient. Planning and preparing for a big shared ritual was a comfort and a high; we social humans love being actively involved in a common purpose. One such ritualistic activity was preparing for the sacrificial ritual of mass murder (war).

Leslie—Are you saying that if people become very worried, even obsessively worried, together in a group, they then sometimes begin compulsive rituals together?

Irene—Well, most of the time people have other things on their mind than purity. Friends and larger groups meet together, gossip together, share stories together, discuss economic developments, throw around political ideas, etc. in what has become known as groupthink. When people began to think together or worry together as a group, there were technical terms to describe the phenomenon as "entrainment (synchronization) of cortical activity", but even today exactly how this happens is not fully understood.

What is known is what often happened when the intense discussion of the group was about shared very bad political news. If, as a result of that discussion, the members decided to submerge themselves together into some kind of a new joint project, the level of anxiety in the community would be decreased. Moving together toward a planned major sacrificial ritualistic project such as war added significant cohesion and purpose and meaning to the lives of troubled people. This included the intense involvement of going through the stages of the Dance of Death. Group rituals are group therapy for human communities, still today!

Leslie—How are those rituals of war related to contamination or lack of purity?

Irene—Purity meant different things in different societies. Purity was used politically to mean "homogeneous." Since the absolutely overwhelming majority of the 3.1 billion nucleic acid building blocks (nucleotides) of the human genome are identical between any two people anywhere in the world, only by emphasizing the most miniscule of differences can any specific group of people be thought of as different from any other group. *Prejudice was overwhelmingly based on culture, not biology.*

Groups of people living inside an otherwise homogenous society who had different religions or different customs, gay people, handicapped people, even eccentric people could have been considered polluting members of traditional shame societies.

Leslie—What are shame societies?

<u>Irene</u>—There is going to be more about shame societies tomorrow. The point of this lecture was that those members of such a society who were classified as minorities often were on the defensive; they had a taint of "impurity"; they could become the target of prejudice. At times of crisis and war, such members of these groups were at risk inside their own societies and might have been chosen for scapegoating.

Leslie—I know my history; a lot of ancient wars were related to religious differences; were these fights over purity?

Irene—Differences inside religious groups were particularly dangerous in primitive times. Many of the arguments between the various groups were about purity, being morally superior. Just as the Catholics and Protestants fought it out in Christian Europe, the Sunni and Shia branches of Islam took up arms against each other soon after they were established. For the Salafi form of Sunni Islam, the Shia were even more despised than Jews and Christians. Purity was also a big issue in certain secular societies, such as the Communist infighting over who was a better Marxist.

Leslie—What did the lecturer mean by *purity-maintenance*?

Irene—Just as individuals struggle to keep their food and houses as clean as possible, in primitive times a body politic could use religious organizations in their society to reinforce and defend the purity of their group. Although it was not true of all religious groups in primitive times, a fundamental task of many religions was *purity-maintenance*. Each group of people was unique; historically each had had its own particular impurity/purity focus and fantasies.

Each group had its own way of depersonalizing the "impure" other groups. The amazing variety of documented fantasies was a sad comment on the immense power of the human imagination. In most societies there were a regular number of religious rituals designed to rid each group of its type of pollution. Specially designated individuals (religious leaders) focused on acting out those special religious rites for the group, while everyone else attends more casually to the everyday anti-pollution rituals for individuals such as washing and bathing customs.

Leslie—But doesn't history tell us that *purity-maintenance* by religious leaders wasn't enough in so many societies; that the cleansing power of human blood (wars) was needed to maintain purity?

Irene—Very good! When wars were fought in the name of religion, purification was the stated goal. In English history during the seventeenth century, the religious "pure"-tans (Puritans) were out to impose their specific concepts of religious purity on their own society—as well as neighboring nations—by Oliver Cromwell's bloody wars. His personal motto was doubletalk; it was *Pax Quaeritur Bello* or Peace=War. This concept of war as purifying was still around in England in the twentieth century AD when the Bishop of London made a famous statement during World War I "As I have said a thousand times, I look upon it as a war for purity."

The Army of the Pure, a militant Islamic group that battled the Indian rule of Kashmir, was quite overt about its psychological goal at the end of the twentieth century.[3] In the same time period, the training manual for another Moslem group, the Al-Qaeda had "purification of the ranks of Islam from the elements of depravity" as one of its three goals. In Islam, a body must be washed before burial for purity reasons, but an exception is made for suicide martyrs whose bodies are considered so pure that they do not need to be washed, as they ascend straight to paradise. This is further example of the general principle that blood washes away impurities.

Leslie—I thought that the Middle Ages was the time in Europe when people were overtly focused on religious issues such as moral superiority, holiness, and purity of thought, not the historical periods after that.

Irene—Yes, the Middle Ages were such a time, but later on it was the same subject matter, just more disguised. For example, the various groups of Marxists were focused on purifying their Communist ideologies. The Nazis tried to purify bloodlines. Some of the most horrible mass murders of the twentieth century were done in the name of a politically pure (Communist) society and a racially pure (Nazi) master race.

Humans have always been very susceptible to propaganda about achieving a morally superior society. In the case of the Communists during the twentieth century, they attacked the highly exploitative societies of the industrial revolution and promised fairness to the workers and peasants. But as is characteristic of illusionary utopias, there immediately was the danger of contamination and lack of purity, leading quickly to killing and war. One can make the argument that the enormously successful use of such noble language about a supposedly "classless society" (which fooled millions) softened even the historical understanding of the crimes the Communist leadership committed in many countries during the twentieth century.[4]

Leslie—How about the American Declaration of Independence in 1776 which declared that all people were created equal; that certainly was a utopian statement.

Irene—Yes, what is fascinating is that this utopian ideal was actually an attempt to move beyond purity and homogeneity and all forms of superiority between humans, moral and otherwise. If everyone is equal, no one is superior. But, like Athenian democracy, it was a very limited in practice; the same people who celebrated the Declaration of Independence also wrote the Constitution of the United States where the practice of slavery was assumed and accounted for in the voting provisions of that Constitution. (This was one of the reasons that some of the members of the Constitutional Convention from Virginia and Massachusetts refused to sign that Constitution [5]).

In fact, it took another two generations in the United States before the issue of slavery was finally addressed. Civil wars have an intensity born of intimacy; the president's own wife had family on the Confederate side. The American Civil War became a classic of killing over purity. Ostensibly fought over the issue of states' rights versus national unity, it quickly developed into a war of purifying violence fought over the sin [the impurity] of slavery. One side had hundreds of thousands of slaves (sins) and the other side soon became convinced of its absolute moral superiority—a very deadly combination. A great deal of violence was needed to be adequately purifying.

In fact the bloodiest day in the history of the United States was the battle of Antietam during the Civil War (23,100 killed, wounded or missing). The battle of Gettysburg, where the Devil's Den creek actually ran red because of the amount of blood in it, also did a lot of purifying. In fact, there were so many wars with heavy causalities in primitive times that creeks turning red with blood or being blocked by dead bodies were recorded all over the world. An example from Asia was the Sui river actually ceasing to flow in China in 205 BC due to the number of bodies of officers and soldiers in the river during fight which led to the fall of the Ch'in Dynasty. [6]

Leslie—It is hard to believe that human beings could be so destructive to each other! Didn't anybody figure out what was going on?

Irene—The human race learned very slowly from its encounters with self-imposed violence. An early learner was an American named Oliver Wendell Holmes. His understanding that absolute moral certainty, the belief in moral superiority, may lead to horrible violence was a lesson that he took away from his experience in the Civil War. [7]

Leslie—In any community, how is it decided what is pure and what isn't?

Irene—Like beauty, purity is in the eye of the beholder. The Gypsies in Europe during primitive times were an example of how each society has its own unique purity identity. While Gypsies were thought of as dirty and unclean by the European peoples among whom they traveled, the Gypsies themselves had the same negative opinion of the people around them. Gypsies had a way of life, controlled by ritual purity, which was called *ramanipen* or *romahija,* and had very strict rules governing one's state of personal cleanliness which included restrictions upon contact with other people and animals, the washing of the body, clothing, and dishes as well as the preparation of food. [8] The rest of the people among whom they lived, the Gadze or non-Gypsies, were regarded as unclean since they did not observe these restrictions and could defile Gypsies simply by contact. This may help explain why the Gypsies tended to remain such an outsider group in each society that they entered.

Leslie—But the Gypsies must have been extreme in their point of view, in keeping groups separated from their neighbors.

Irene—Unfortunately, this kind of thinking could be found everywhere. Here read this quote from a poet called T.S. Eliot at the University of Virginia in 1933.

Leslie reads:

> The population should be homogeneous; where two or more cultures exist in the same place they are likely to be either fiercely self-conscious or both become adulterated. What is still more important is unity of religious background; reasons of race and religion combine to make any large number of free-thinking Jews undesirable.[9]

Leslie—I thought T.S. Eliot was a great poet.

Irene—Prejudice and chauvinism are not limited to the illiterate. The attempt to keep a nation "homogenous" requires strong boundaries and the power to enforce them. The more a group is focused on purity, the greater the drive for power designed to maintain those strong psychological boundaries. Violence does not lag far behind, enforcing one of the most destructive variations of the power and boundary issue. In Europe, the "pollution" of economic migrants from the third world brought the homogeneity/purity issue to the surface of politics at the beginning of the twenty-first century. Jean-Marie le Pen, an extreme right-winger, took second place in the 2002 French presidential race. He is quoted as having said "Youths need purity. From this point of view, the SS with its uniform is a bit like the priest in his cassock". [10]

The concept of purity used politically as "homogenous" or religiously as "orthodox" reveals its conservative tone. Since all life—including human life—changes over time and can not remain static, the rigid ideals of purity eventually became a truly backward force in any society where they were practiced.

"Morally superior" people considered their reactionary ideology worth fighting for because, in their eyes, others were morally bankrupt. This attempt to maintain the self-identity of a group as "morally superior and pure" had many bad spin-offs. If the group's moral superiority appears threatened, a common bad spin-off was war. In these cases the Dance of Death partner often was another "morally superior"-obsessed society also struggling with issues of purity.

Leslie—Back to my previous question—surely there were many people, many leaders, who tried to change the stifling atmosphere of depersonalization of slaves or ethnic cleansing of scapegoats during periods when such intense purity-seeking was going on.

Irene—Of course there were many such individuals of conscience, but leaders who acted against the trends of their times were much rarer.

It is so interesting that apparently the key was that these leaders focused on taking care of their own personal needs first instead of conforming to the cultures in which they lived; in that sense they played to their own tune; they even could have been acting in ways that others perceived as morally inferior, living like *bon vivants*. Do you want to hear about a story from Nazi Europe?

Leslie—yes.

Irene—A scandalous *bon vivant* who took action to stop sacrificial shedding of blood was the German industrialist Oscar Schindler, who was a member of the Nazi party. He personally saved many Jewish lives in the midst of the Nazi Holocaust of Jews.[11]

Leslie—So you are saying that being selfish and somewhat immune to the group culture could be a good thing? I thought that people alienated from the group tended to be psychopaths.

Irene—That is one possibility. But actually, during World War II in Nazi-occupied Europe, there were a few people who felt intact enough about themselves to resist group intimidation and do what Schindler did—saving innocent Jewish lives.

Leslie—That reminds me of something I wanted to ask you—I learned in history that after World War II ended, some of the states in Europe involved in that huge war went through several decades afterwards with few or no wars; what kind of communities were they?

Irene—Well, you can argue that their need for blood sacrifice, their sacrificial quotient, had been fully used up by such a mighty war. But actually those rare cases of societies who tended to move away from war in primitive times were likely to be "impure" societies run by relaxed leaders—communities where having a good time was celebrated. These societies tended to tolerate ethnic diversity, improved rights for women, sexual ambiguity and their eccentric, weirdest members.

Moralists, on the other hand, filled up primitive history with spectacular failures with ugly endings, from Robespierre of the French Revolution to the Taliban of Afghanistan. In primitive times many societies would go through cycles when each group had an overwhelming need to feel as pure as possible; the group simply had to have its honor—that is, lack of shame. Honor was achieved in each nation by its own particular customs, but to be viewed as honorable was a universal necessity for each group. Just as shamed individuals may enter upon a narcissistic pursuit of perfection to conceal their shame, groups suffering from shame may pursue a form of group narcissism known as jingoism. In primitive times, it was best to *beware the [shamed] super-patriot.*

Leslie—This is all too depressing.

Irene—It is even worse than that. The fanatic focus on purity by a society can result in genocide. Whether it was the American colonists killing the last 20 Susquehanna Indians in 1763 or the German Nazis exterminating 6 million Jews in Europe by 1945, this deliberate extermination of human life is the same deadly behavior seen over and over again based on the *depersonalization of the impure*. One of the best ways to prepare for total exploitation of a group of subjugated people leading to human blood sacrifices was to depersonalize that group of people by considering them filthy and impure.

Ok, enough; no more; it's time for the next lecture.

Chapter 10

▼

Shame Societies & Guilt Societies

Abstract 1010—Shame societies/guilt societies

Criteria to identify a shame society

- The highest value to respect in someone is purity and piety; ideological leaders and pious politicians are greatly honored.

- There is an emphasis on life after death and suspicion of fun in this life.

- There is a strong need for the society to be perceived as morally superior, to the point of projecting and blaming other groups for its own faults. Thus, there often is a strong drive to impose its values and its ideology on other groups.

- The society is extremely hierarchical; men have the economic, political, and religious power and enforce their privileges to the detriment of women. The natural beauty of women often is considered threatening.

- The majority of women agree to rules set by men and help men enforce them; their role is often limited to being mistresses, servants and incubators of men's children.

- Class structure is pronounced. There can be *de jure* or *de facto* slavery in such societies.

- In spite of a tradition of hospitality to strangers, members of other groups who live among them are kept separate and never really accepted. Prejudice toward members of minorities is considered a natural way of thinking.

- Power based on violence is seen as a normal way for political problem-solving.

- The political leadership, particularly during times of war, may arise from the criminal element of the society.

- The state feels free to commit sadism from time to time.

- The sacrificial quotient includes more violence and war and less altruism.

Criteria to identify a guilt society

- Feelings of moral superiority arise from real-life group altruism rather than theoretical religious or ideological precepts.

- The majority agree to keep church and state separate.

- There is an emphasis on achievement in this world rather than in the next. Artists who push limits, while upsetting many, nevertheless are protected and valued.

- The presence of hierarchy everywhere in the society is diminished.

- Women become independent or full partners rather than servants and incubators.

- The drive of a guilt society to impose its values on other societies is blunted.

- Toleration of people and values from alternate lifestyles within the community is a goal. Toleration of people and values from other completely separate communities is another goal. To be prejudiced is considered a fault.

- The society struggles to take responsibility for its actions and not project the blame too unfairly.

- Violence is the last, not the first, method for political problem-solving.

- There is such abhorrence of sadism that the society can not use torture.

- The sacrificial quotient includes less violence and war and more altruism.

Leslie—(sigh) I haven't yet fully digested the concept from the last lecture of *depersonalization of the impure.* Now there are these twin lectures on shame societies and guilt societies during primitive times; I could think of so many examples as I was listening.

Irene—You know your history!

Leslie—But I can tell you one thing I didn't understand at all in that lecture—it was the statement that, although the feelings of shame and guilt are based on social norms shaped by each distinct culture, they can be consistently characterized across cultures.

Irene—Yes, that has been shown by many studies; feeling shame and guilt are primary normal human emotions that evolved from prototypes found in other primates and can be characterized in individuals no matter what society they belong to. This has been demonstrated both historically and cross-culturally [1]

Leslie—Do we know the physiological basis of shame and guilt?

Irene—We are still working on the details of how the human brain works, but it appears that genes related to the internal experiences of shame are derived from submissive strategies in other primates [2].

Incidentally, it is not just emotions that can be identified across cultures, certain aberrant human behavior patterns that are clearly abnormal, such as sociopathy or psychopathy, have core manifestations that are stable and can be recognized with a combination of clinical and laboratory studies [3][4]

Leslie—Wait a minute—I thought you didn't like the theories, philosophical or scientific, that tried to identify universal principles of human behavior based on deductive observations. That you thought morality was a set of customs and values slightly different for each cultural group. This negates the idea of absolute moral values! Isn't that what you told me?

Irene—Yes, but …

Leslie—And furthermore I remember that you pointed out to me that killing was a good example of this lack of absolutes, since, although our modern society abhors all killing, in primitive times entire communities went around imitating the bizarre people who are the killers—creating wars at regular intervals and practicing capital punishment.

Irene—So?

Leslie—Look. I already know a lot about shame (the feeling of public exposure) and guilt (the private, internal emotion). I admit that what I didn't know was what the twentieth century primitives had already discovered that these two emotions, they had <u>opposite effects</u> on violence, as shown by studies in criminals [5]. It was fascinating that increasing shame and public humiliation are the conditions most likely to turn a person toward violent acting out while increasing guilt had the opposite effect.

Increase the shame and violence increases; increase the guilt and violence diminishes!

Irene—Right; this was such an important finding back then; it has led to our contemporary approach in curtailing killing. Because with certain caveats, this insight about individuals is of value in understanding the behavior of groups; Sigmund Freud, who invented psychohistory in the twentieth century, wrote that the heightening of a sense of guilt was most important in the evolution of a culture.

Leslie—Wait a minute; this is a question I had—if guilt is a private feeling, how can it be relevant to the group?

Irene—In the right political hands, it can be a technique to make the members of the opposing group feel guilty as their own group behaves badly toward another group. The great leaders of the twentieth century, like Mahatma Gandhi of India and Nelson Mandela of South Africa, avoided bloodshed by using guilt-inducing tactics against their imperialist enemies.

Leslie—Just a minute; I thought the twentieth century was an unusually bloody century convulsed by a number of extreme shame societies of the fascist type[6].

Irene—You are touching on a sore point for the theorists of shame societies and guilt societies. The ones who first proposed these concepts were so blinded by incredible color prejudice that what they proposed was backward—that the nations of white people, many of which had become fascistic in the first half of the twentieth century, were the guilt societies while the nations of dark-skinned people where Gandhi and Mandela worked were shame societies [7].

Leslie—But during the twentieth century, societies weren't fixed; didn't they swing back and forth between these two styles?

Irene—Yes, states had an internal mixture of the two types and could shift in balance between them as a dominant theme. This creates the shame/guilt variable for each group. For the twentieth century, Denmark was a good example of this fluidity. During World War II, the people of Denmark as a group saved their minority Jewish citizens from the Nazi death camps—using the cover of night, they shipped the Jews to nearby Sweden under the very noses of the Nazis. This was truly a splendid guilt-society action! Yet by the end of the century, during the prelude to the second Gulf War, the Danes were the only group of people in the European Union who favored a war in Iraq; even the British whose leaders had taken them into the war rejected the violence by majorities in opinion polls. The descendants of the noble Danes of the twentieth century moved toward a shame society in the twenty-first.

Leslie—I'm not clear about a lot of this; let's go back to the basics. Please explain how an individual feeling shame can be translated into a whole society of shame. I know for the individual it is about being seen by others as impure, tainted in some way, and that primitive men sometimes fought bloody duels between each other to wash away that shame.

Irene—Both twentieth century French and the classical Greek language had two words for shame, connoting respectively a more private or a more public sense. The word *pudeur* in French was associated with a personal covering up of sexual matters; *honte* referred to the loss of honor in the eyes of others. It is in the latter sense that shame is applied here to the concept of shame societies.

You are right that impurity is the underlying feeling that drives shame societies. "Saving face", that is avoiding shame, has been found as a major theme in those societies. They were obsessed with moral superiority/purity as an ideal that required constant vigilance against impurity. It was indeed hard to ward off all the threats to purity that the natural ambiguous reality of life presented! This produced the need for continuous rituals controlling as much of life as possible.

Leslie—The lecturer said that they were particularly hard on women.

Irene—That's an understatement. In the twentieth century, in states catering to religious extremism, there were many examples of men interfering with women's rights, even their bodies. In Pakistan, in 1979, a law was passed called the Hudood ordinance; if a woman reported being raped, she could end up being prosecuted for adultery. This law led to the punishment of thousands of innocent women. In the twentieth century in the United States, in the states dominated by the religious right, both men and women, needing to feel morally superior, wanted to interfere when a girl needed to make the unfortunate decision to have an abortion.

Leslie—It is hard to imagine the personality of people who lived in such kill-joy societies, and put up with such an intrusive group ritualistic life as the lecturer described today. Is it true that the Taliban of Afghanistan didn't even allow children to play by flying kites?

Irene—Alas, yes. The rigidity of such societies is based on absolutes, including attempts to exclude the inevitable movement of ideas and people. Shame societies are cultures where people are not allowed to experience their own anger directly, but get it out in group packaging as moral, righteous indignation—that is, by feeling morally superior.

Leslie—So if shame societies were so focused on being superior and perfect, why were they so prone to violence? To bloodletting? To war?

Irene—It might be because it is impossible to maintain a homeostasis of perfect morality, leaving such societies in constant need of being "purified." Prewar maneuvers, the Dance of Death, would begin by two such communities focusing exclusively on each other and verbally attacking and shaming each other. They were helping each other dance toward the inevitable blood sacrifice that both societies needed in order to become "pure" again. Preparing for war, the group became a wonderful sponge absorbing the misery and anger and hatred of its members as it prepared to squeeze them out again in community-directed focused lethal form.

Leslie—What about the people in the guilt societies of the twentieth century; didn't they have wars too?

Irene—Avoidance of war was much more likely to occur in guilt societies, where societies had moved forward, giving up enough purity and moral superiority to leave behind the shame society model. These were communities which could tolerate ambiguity and differences rather than focusing on homogenous purity. It was not that they had given up bad feelings; whole societies felt guilty together; they had a "guilty groupthink". But they tended to handle their group negative feelings in a different way—by developing other ways of meeting their sacrificial needs in forms other than blood sacrifice.

For individuals, guilt or self-reproach is the inner experience of a bad conscience over breaking one's own rules. But humans are very social mammals, and it is not just what we do ourselves that induces guilt. We can suffer guilt through an act of identification with other people, even those we never knew. For example, a specific effect of catastrophes like war or genocide is *survivor guilt* suffered by the surviving individuals even though they had absolutely no responsibility for the deaths of their fellow victims [8]. These people feel guilty for merely being alive; this is an example of how many humans feel profoundly group-identified, even in the most unlikely of situations.

Leslie—Give me an example of a group of people meeting their sacrificial needs in a form other than blood sacrifice?

Irene—If you didn't fall asleep this afternoon, you might have heard the lecturer give the example of Serbia and the Netherlands as a shame-guilt society interaction. Although the Serbians, then a shame society, organized and massacred more than 6,000 unarmed Moslem men and boys of Srebrenica in 1995, apparently it was the people of the Netherlands who suffered the guilt. At the time of the massacre, the Dutch undermanned and lightly armed UN peacekeepers were taken hostage by the Serbian army, leaving the Moslems in the wrong-named "safe area" to their fate. This haunted the country of the Netherlands and eventually led to the resignation of the Prime Minister Wim Kok and his cabinet; when resigning he said "The Netherlands has to take its share of that responsibility." By personally assuming some of the guilt and resigning because of it, prime minister Kok performed the nonlethal sacrifice of the leader for his guilt-oriented society.

Leslie—Are you implying that guilt societies take responsibilities for their actions, even if the apparent evil doing of their group was totally inadvertent?

Irene—Yes, just like *survivor guilt*, there can be no exact responsibility. It's a human group identity issue. Guilt societies struggle over the full meaning of their inadvertent yet unacceptable actions and try to fathom their own possible motives. They are suffering and need to be purged by a sacrifice. But, because blood sacrifice has become unacceptable to them (usually including a ban on capital punishment), nonlethal forms of sacrifice were developed—often economic or sometimes political, as in the Dutch case. By the twenty-first century, the Dutch soldiers, even in extreme war zones, were concentrating on way to avoid the act of killing, if at all possible.[9]

Leslie—I admit I fell asleep. And I know I missed the end of the lecture which discussed "good wars", so I'll ask you now where that puzzling concept of "goodness" came from in situations where people were deliberately murdering each other.

Irene—In primitive times, the idea that war could be positive, a "good" war or a "just" war, was discussed from St. Augustine to the writers of the United Nations Charter. It is interesting that shame societies and guilt societies had quite different approaches, yet both could call war good. You must have missed the declaration of an Italian artistic movement called the Futurists at the beginning of the twentieth century. These were an example of extreme shame society types of groups. They said "We will glorify war—the world's only hygiene—militarism, patriotism, beautiful ideas worth dying for, and scorn for women. We will destroy the museums, libraries and academies of every kind, we'll fight feminism, every opportunistic or utilitarian cowardice. We will sing of great crowds excited by their work, by pleasure and by riot".[10] These Italians really were futurists of their own time; they correctly anticipated the important elements of fascism about to engulf Italy, including its glorification of war.

Leslie—Wow! What sick shame societies there were back then! Are you sure that guilt societies also called war good?

Irene—Yes, but for guilt societies, there was not the open embrace of war as a good thing in advance. Religious leaders and diplomats would work sincerely trying to stop the coming war usually during the Dance of Death phrase. For guilt societies, the concept of self-defense often became the ideological justification for a "good" war. War leaders often needed to start up the hostilities by fake attacks and outright lies, as Johnson did at the Gulf of Tonkin starting the Vietnam War.

Leslie—If I got my history right, World War II resulted in a total of up to a hundred million people being killed, if you count the Japanese excursion throughout Asia. The war was a terrible calamity to every group involved, including the Germans; one out of every four of them was killed or wounded. Surely no one called that a "good" war.

Irene—Even that was called a good war by some. It's time for supper; let's go.

CHAPTER 11

▼

ABOUT MEN AND WAR

Abstract 1011 Men are more involved with violence and war than women, but there is a huge spectrum from Genghis Kahn to Albert Schweitzer. In the case of individuals, boys are at higher risk for neurodevelopmental disease and its concomitant behavioral problems. Men with their muscles, hormones and brains are equipped to be killers of animals, but the selection of members of their own species as the victims is a peculiar deviation from other mammalian behavior. In the case of both men and women, the group culture appears to be an overriding factor setting up gender role expectations and warlike behavior.

Leslie—You and I have always had a lot of fun joking about men and women, since I'm a male student and you're a female teacher. But after today's lecture, I wonder if we can joke so much; in fact, some of the archival material on males and war is so extremely blood-thirsty and death-dealing that at first I thought the translations must be wrong.

Irene—It's ok; wait until the next lecture on women and war; there's lots of deadly group behavior in women, too; much of the time, men carried out those acts with women solidly behind them.

Leslie—At least you know that the behavior of men in those primitive days was different from the men of today who live in our nonviolent society. High adventure and sacrifice aren't missing from our lives; we just experience them in nonviolent forms. Our modern culture gives appropriate recognition to the physical strength of us men, an area where we tend to have an edge. The whole world celebrates our intellectual strength, particularly our systemizing abilities. Our communities especially enjoy the compassion and empathy of so many of us men, who successfully compete in those areas too. All this was quite evident among men in primitive times, but I guess that compassion and empathy were never so celebrated and well rewarded back then as the power and boundary games were back then.

Irene—Yes, yes, it's all true. We can talk about contemporary society if you want to change the subject, but it looks like you're trying to avoid going over the material in this lecture on primitive times. I do understand! The subject is quite distasteful, but as archeological historians we have to be aware of it.

Wars in primitive history were about violence and death-dealing, and boys and men in primitive times appeared to be more involved in these topics than girls and women.

Leslie—Alright; let's discuss the lecture; please start with that English study at the end of the twentieth century on gender differences.

Irene—That big study was mentioned in the lecture on individual violence. Now we'll look at another part of that same study; here the investigators were trying to measure the differences in the genders regarding individual violence and antisocial behavior.[1]

That part of the study took place in England, an island with a very low murder rate for primitive times. The English study followed 1,000 males and females from the ages of 3 to 21 years to assess the difference in the sexes regarding individual violence and antisocial behavior. Techniques from developmental psychology, psychiatry, and criminology were used for measurements.

Leslie—I remember from the lecture that males exhibited more physical aggression, theft, and violence than females in every age group!

Irene—Yes, and males outnumbered females 10-to-1 on a life-course of persistent very severe antisocial behavior and violence and had many more multiple poor outcomes as young adults!

Leslie—That's terrible. Did they figure out why that happened?

Irene—Well, they found that the boys had more hyperactivity, more peer pressure problems and more personality traits associated with violent behavior. Most important of all, they found that boys were more likely to have a compromised neuro-cognitive status than girls were.

Leslie—So did they find out whether the gender differences in violence and antisocial behavior were predominantly environmental or predominantly genetic?

Irene—For the individual child with antisocial behavior, this study came down on the side of genetics. Males predominated only because of their greater genetic susceptibility to neurodevelopmental disease entities affecting brain function.

Leslie—I thought men and women had roughly the same amount of serious psychiatric disease, at least as adults.

Irene—They do; this was a study of antisocial personalities.

Leslie—So exactly what did this English study say about men and violence?

Irene—This study was focused on individuals at odds with society and found that neuropsychiatric diseases of developmental origin, which are more common in males, helped explain why antisocial men were more prone to violence. But this study did not explain why men in general were found in so many societies during primitive times to commit more violence and death-dealing than women.

Leslie—OK, but didn't some scholars believe that men in general were more interested in killing and war?

Irene—There was a theory in the twentieth century that contended that killing and war was natural to the male gender, a form of hypermasculine behavior—the extreme male behavior of otherwise normal men.[2] Its author identified the fascination with the technology of killing, especially the complicated technology of modern nuclear and other weapons of mass murder, as a predominantly male interest, a so-called "right-brained" skill.

Leslie—Wait a minute; I think of killing as a highly emotional act—not an intellectual interest.

Irene—Of course you are right; murdering a member of your own species is aggression twisted to meet the need of omnipotence by an act of sadism.

Leslie—Was there evidence of that so-called hypermasculine behavior before the twentieth century?

Irene—Certainly primitive history is replete with episodes of what can only be called extreme male behavior. There were cultures of death, such as the super-heated masculine culture of the Aztecs. This was a society where fathers would kill their sons at 10 years of age if they were suspected of being effeminate.[3]

Leslie—What was life like in such societies?

Irene—All Aztec cities featured racks where skulls were displayed. The Aztecs' life was a frenzy of killing; there were an estimated 20,000 heart extractions alone per year. The Aztecs developed six grizzly varieties of human sacrifice:

1. Heart extraction: priests ripped out a still beating heart from the chest.

2. Immolation: captives thrown alive on burning coals.

3. Beheading followed by defleshing the skull.

4. Sacrifice by arrows, a rite called *Tlacaaliztle*.

5. Sacrifice of children: purchased from obliging parents, they were either drowned or permanently sealed in groups of four inside mountain caves.

6.   Autosacrifice: the entire population might pierce their lips, ears, arms, and legs with thorns collecting blood on paper-like slips to be presented to the gods; royalty and priests pierced tongues and genitals; some priests jumped off high temples to their deaths, while others went into four-year penances before voluntarily submitting to heart extraction.

Leslie—That's almost unbelievable! How could such a murderous society come into being?

Irene—Many historical factors, but the lack of significant cultural input from women might have been one of them

Leslie—Alright, but the Aztecs were quite extreme; how about other less extreme primitive societies where killing and war was celebrated.

Irene—Like the Roman Empire? In Rome, there were several temples to the god Mars. In the center of Rome, there was the Temple of *Mars Ultor*, which means Mars the Avenger.

Leslie—Why was Mars an avenger?

Irene—Because the temple was built to celebrate winning the battle of Philippe, where Augustus and Mark Anthony avenged Julius Caesar's death by defeating his assassins in battle.

Leslie—Who was Mars?

Irene—Mars, known as the King of the Gods, was the Roman god of war and peace. Originally a god of fertility and boundaries, he became associated with fighting, and it was imagined that he preceded the troops into a battlefield. The Romans called themselves the sons of Mars, because they believed him to be the father of Romulus, a legendary founder of Rome. Mars was more widely worshipped than any of the other Roman gods. If the Roman Senate was going to discuss matters of war, it would meet in Temple Mars Ultor. War triumphs were celebrated in this temple.

Leslie—But we do know from history that, although Rome was a very male military and hierarchical society, wasn't there a kind of Roman peace in the conquered areas, a peace based on trading rather than on endless war?

Irene—Right, also this was not such an exclusive male society as that of the Aztecs; there was even a little worship of women from the imperial families mixed into the culture.

Leslie—Speaking of women, let's go back to the causes of violence in the lecture. What about men competing over female mates; didn't that cause violence?

Irene—During primitive times, there were evolutionary psychologists who believed that the violent patterns of human male behavior were based on obtaining reproductive advantage—that is, competing with other males for females. They based this theory on the fact that the armies often consisted mostly of the unmarried young men (still in the process of finding a mate) and that the weapons of war, from the simplest sword to the cruise missile, were clearly phallic symbols. This competitive drive was thought to be a human variation on animal behavior who fight over mates. But that was based on misinformation; it is now known that most vertebrates and invertebrates don't fight each other to the death in that situation; the loser makes a stereotyped gesture of submission and leaves.

Leslie—But aren't men, with their muscles and hormones, equipped to be killers?

Irene—Yes, of course, like many male mammals, men are equipped with muscles and hormones and the brain power to be killers of animals of other species, the ones that they then choose to eat. Our cousins, the Neanderthals, were particularly well muscled and big meat-eaters. Although there is to this day a great interest in testosterone, the male hormone, and how it might affect the capacity for violence in our species, it is not the ability to make a kill which needs examination. The ability to kill successfully is a given for humans.

It is the selection of the victim that needs a better explanation. The bottom line is this—why would a social species like human beings start killing each other in addition to animal prey?

Leslie—Yes, I understand, it is the selection of human, rather than animal, victims for which our killing skills are made. Our hormones give us power.

Irene—As you well know, hormones also exist for sexual activity. There was a belief during primitive times in the role that the hormones of sexual activity played in violence. There are a number of papers in primitive times that blamed the hormone testosterone for what was labeled the *pseudosexuality of violence*. The late adolescents who filled the ranks of an army in primitive times certainly had plenty of testosterone which might have accounted for the proxy-passion of violence. In the Hungarian language, the words for killing (ölés) and embracing (ölelés) echo and heighten each other. Aristophanes, an ancient Greek playwright, explored that special relationship between sexuality and war in his play Lysistrata, where wives withheld sex until the men stopped fighting. However based on our understanding of neurophysiology, it is likely that Aristophanes got it backwards—if anything, decreasing sex may increase violence. As abused wives in primitive times would testify, a man temporarily unable to perform sexually sometimes might substitute violence.

Irene—I have to admit that I am fascinated by the eroticism of violence.

Leslie—You are not the only one. There are a large number of literary artifacts of the joke variety describing swords and guns as penis extensions. The Nazis raised an arm to salute Hitler in imitation of a stiff penis. The intermingling of killing with male ejaculation during war was discussed in the psychoanalytic literature. The following eroticized violence[4] was recorded during the war between the United States and Vietnam, a war that went on from 1965-1973:

   a. Helicopter door gunners with erections while firing;

   b. Rangers on ambush ejaculating at the sight of an enemy "exploding";

   c. Paratroopers ejaculating while jumping;

   d. Exploding detonation caps inside the genitals of captured North Vietnamese Army nurses;

   e. Stuffing enemy genitals inside the mouths of dead soldiers.

Leslie—It makes one wonder if killing is the strongest of all the passions!

Irene—Indeed!

Leslie—So is there any understanding of how these horrors could happen?

Irene—Well, if one puts together all the evidence in primitive times from both the common warlike societies and the rare peaceful ones, there is some vague idea of what caused them. Neither animal behavior nor fighting over a mate nor innate hormone levels appeared to account for the level of violence of the men of any particular community. Actually in the case of both men and women, *the group culture appeared to be the overriding factor* that sets up the gender role expectations and the warlike behavior.

Leslie—Did everyone go along?

Irene—Unfortunately, history suggests that almost everyone went along as the killing increased in any given society. The first Emperor of China (258-210 BC) changed the previous rules which were protecting the life of prisoners of war; in an early war, he ordered all of them killed—10,000 at a time. Just like that. He killed many more in the process of building the 3000 mile Great Wall of China.

Not that there weren't men who defied the group expectations in primitive times, as shown by pacifist movements on all the continents. These were men, motivated by religion, a horror of killing others or rational self-interest, who flatly refused to enter the killer/victim scenario of military service. But they were tiny in actual number.

Leslie—So what happened to the overwhelming majority who did enter military service?

Irene—It is hard to understand, from our modern point of view, the type of military training of primitive times to which the young man apparently voluntarily would submit himself. As the lecturer emphasized several times, overall it was designed to prevent the young soldier from defending himself; these young men were carefully trained to follow orders from their leader in blind obedience. The basic training of armies was designed to strip the soldier of his individuality developed throughout his childhood by his parents, particularly what his mother taught him. The training was designed to make him as much as possible like a robot who would immediately follow an order without a second thought. On the battlefield, these orders could include entering an enemy area where the young soldier had a real chance of being wounded or killed.

Leslie—So soldiers had to lose their individuality?

Irene—In war situations, there was more to it than just not thinking as an individual; in primitive times, armies actually had to consist of deluded people. In order to be effective at their job of murdering and overcome their inborn empathy, the members of an army had to profoundly demonize and dehumanize their enemy. This was a fundamental of any army in primitive times.

Another important illusion of each army was that they were magical winners who could not be stopped. If that fantasy began to falter, it could become a very dangerous time during a war; when group self-esteem went down, group cruelty and violence could go up. Since each war, like any contest, had its winners and losers, half of the armies were bound to be in that dangerous losing position.

Leslie—What happened to the half of the armies who were on the losing side?

Irene—As you imagine, their group esteem starts to go way down; they had endured so much only to be on the losing side. This creates the need to diminish those bad feelings, often by compensatory group violent behavior. Losing armies can be very dangerous indeed!

Leslie—Give me examples.

Irene—In World War II, the Nazi-led German army began to lose first on the eastern front and then on the western front. The defeat at Stalingrad on the eastern front started an increase in murder of the remaining Jewish people—old people, women, children—in the occupied territories by the Nazi SS troops. [5]

On the western front, shortly after the Allied troops landed successfully at Normandy, Nazi SS troops encircled in the village of Oradour-sur-Glane in the French countryside and killed the inhabitants. The men were marched off to barns and shot; the women and children locked into a church and set on fire. [6]

Leslie—Enough! How could men in the twentieth century be part of such behavior?

Irene—Although we think of conscript soldiers as victims of their group, as *the blood of the beloved*, it was not that clear in primitive times. Then there were many men in both the upper and lower ranks who apparently enjoyed being in the army. Human beings are social and enjoy group activities; for many boys, it may have represented the first adult socialization away from their family. Enjoying the comradeship that develops within the army, the forced closeness developed new kinds of male social pleasures. Being human, many men were comfortable in a hierarchical organization.

If one asked them, the boys and men who joined an army, particularly in time of peril, often reported an altruistic reason—to protect and help their group, to please their family. Just like everyone else they wanted to make their contribution to the community and feel the warmth that comes from social good. Most human beings have a drive to lend meaning to their life; at some level soldiers may have rationalized that to take a chance of dying for the group gave their death (an inevitable development someday anyway!) a special meaning.

Leslie—Are you sure that some men liked being in the army?

Irene—For sure; apparently some men loved the excitement and danger of war and preferred it to the relative dullness of a civilian life as it was lived out in primitive times (not like our modern age, which is full of adventure games). War at that time celebrated youthful strength and power; to some of these men, war was the climax of human existence. This was particularly true of the generals and higher ranking officers with power of ordering men to their deaths. A World War II general, General George S. Patton, famously said "Compared to war, all other forms of human endeavor shrink into insignificance. God, I do love it so." But this love was not limited to professional soldiers. There were many testimonies by drafted men who returned to civilian life after a war, and later reported that their war experience was "the highlight of their lives".[7]

You heard the lecturer report on the American soldier wounded in Iraq, during the US-Iraq conflict of the twenty-first century, who said:

> "It was like, 'Wow, man, I was born for the Army. I was an adrenaline junkie. I was super, super fit. I craved discipline. I wanted adventure. I was patriotic. I loved the bonding. And there was nothing I was feared of. I mean, man, I was made for war.'"[8]

Leslie—We all like to be part of groups, but why do they have to be part of killing machines?

Irene—Of course, they don't have to be. In primitive times, it was this allure of group participation *fraught with danger* that allowed men to subsume their own personalities to the group and to become devoted comrades, ready to take on the task of the group whatever it happened to be. The exact ideology was mostly just a cover. History saw that in Indian/Chinese wars at the middle of the twenty-first century when there were huge numbers of excessive males in both countries.

It was this combination of loyalty and competition among a cohesive group of males, all armed with death-dealing weapons, which led to so much horror in primitive times.

Leslie—But you still haven't answered why it was the boys, rather than the girls, who did the killing. Girls like to be part of groups, too.

Irene—Well, here is a theory that is kicking around about why men themselves in primitive times were so often associated with killing. A deep psychological reason why such male-dominated cultures may have been so oriented toward death could be that killing is the only chance for men to feel as powerful as gods. It was their only chance to actually directly affect life and death—in the case of men, limited to death. *Wishing for omnipotence is very human.*

The sensation of creating life is impossible for men to experience directly, and must be left to their wives when they give birth. It could be argued that a powerful influence in many cultures in primitive times was hidden male envy of females and their ability to produce children [9], even though men are aware that their sperm is an essential factor at the start of the process. In fact, it could be said that war (killing life) is the male's triumph over the female's (lifegiving) process of giving birth.

Leslie—I think that idea is ridiculous.

Irene—It may seem ridiculous to you, but there were quite a number of artifacts from primitive times suggesting that men wished to be the creators of life. A scholar reported that in the earliest times, there was "the primitive awe felt by men towards women as possessed of divine creative power in their ability to bear children".[10] The psychoanalysts of the twentieth century AD called this phenomenon "parturition envy". Many of the primitive cultures had myths of creator males. An ancient Egyptian myth, written in hieroglyphics, has the male god Atum saying "I created my own being—my fist became my spouse." Other examples were the Hittite god Kumarbi swallowing the semen of his castrated father and thus conceiving the goddess of love within his own body, as well as the ancient Greek god Zeus creating Athena from his head. In the Judeo-Christian tradition, it was a male God that created Eve from Adam's rib.

Leslie—Do you know an archeology paper that shows that the story of Adam and Eve was a borrowing from the polytheistic culture of the Sumerians. EDIN was a word in the Sumerian language for cultivated field or garden, transformed by the Hebrew language into the biblical garden of EDEN. But most interesting was the Sumerian play on words—TI.L (life) and TI (rib) are virtually the same word. Oblivious to the original Sumerian play on words, the Hebrews applied the concrete interpretation of creating life from a rib.

Irene—No, I didn't know that one, perhaps it's not surprising that one of the first stories in monotheism historically comes from polytheism. However it does appear that the concept of monotheism—one male god who was the creator of all life—actually was an elaboration of the magical fantasy of a male creator.

During later primitive times, there also was the less overt and therefore more acceptable fantasy of being "twice born" or "born again" through the agency of a male god following the undeniable fact of the birth from a female the first time around. What is so fascinating to us today is that most women living in societies dominated by monotheistic religions went along with this peculiar male fantasy that a male god can be a solitary "creator" without female help.

Leslie—Can you explain how that happened?

Irene—Not really; at the time, it was suggested that perhaps the females were using the psychological defense mechanism of "identifying with the aggressor", but actually I have no idea.

Leslie—Besides fantasies about male gods, did groups of men ever pretend to create babies?

Irene—Actual examples of males acting out their need to have the power of god-like creation of life was found in many primitive artifacts, as in Argentina during the 1976-1983 military junta.[11,12] Officially an anti-left campaign, hundreds of people were killed and part of the project degenerated into a vicious scheme targeting pregnant women. The hapless young pregnant women were captured and held prisoner until their babies were born, the infants were taken from them and some of the mothers were thrown into the ocean, their abdomens cut open bleeding to attract sharks. Then the infants were adopted, sometimes by the very people who had murdered their mothers—usually policemen's families, military families or other families of the ruling junta.

Thus the grandiose Argentinean military males, who also were the main instigators of the Falkland war, "created" babies. (Thanks to DNA, some of these babies many years later were reclaimed by their grandparents or other members of their birth families.) Were these men imitating a similar phenomenon, on a lesser scale, which occurred during the Spanish Civil War? In that case Franco's male "social workers" snatched babies and small children from left-wing families and gave them to his supporters.[13]

Leslie—History is really depressing. I am glad that I live today; how were we able to stop all this crazy stuff?

Irene—As you know very well, in our modern times, we have channeled the group excitement and energy that used to be used up in wars into many other effective substitutes, including all known variations of competitive games. It was realized even in primitive times that competitive sporting events drained off some of the partisanship and aggression of a group. The ancient Greeks invented the Olympics (776 BC), stopping any war going on at the time to honor these athletic competitions. It was for males only. In ancient Rome, almost everyone was a fan of either the Blues or the Greens, the two main teams of charioteers. However fans of the opposite sides often spilled blood as well; once a terrible riot occurred between the two partisan groups which eventually had to be stopped by armed troops; the deaths were in the hundreds.

Nevertheless, it is a historical fact that during primitive times, sporting events in themselves clearly were not adequate for meeting the fundamental needs for wars and human blood sacrifice by groups. Often sports were interim substitutes to be played until it was time for the real thing.

Leslie—The next lecture is on women and war in historical times; I wonder what we are going to find out there.

———— ▼ ————

CHAPTER 12

ABOUT WOMEN AND WAR

Abstract 1012 In primitive times, buildings (mostly the creation and work of men) were more important than people (mostly the lifework of women). That mothers allowed their sons to become shooting targets and trained killers as soldiers was strong proof of the overriding appeal of group identity/ideology over all other gender, environmental and genetic predispositions. Some females were involved in war, first as war goddesses and later as women warriors. Women were often the targets of taboos for fear of their contaminating the group. In the case of both men and women, group culture tended to be the overriding factor setting up gender roles and violent behavior.

Leslie—You know I had difficulty with the last lecture on men and war, but this one on women and war is even harder for me to digest. It is really hard for me to understand how the mothers of the historically primitive periods could go along with turning their own children into shooting targets and trained killers during wars.

Irene—You are talking about thousands of years of mothers; no one knows the answer. There is the impression, as it appears to the historical scholars, of the utter political powerlessness of women, particularly mothers. They were at the bottom of the hierarchies. You would think the evidence would be greatest in the early nonliterate primitive period, when muscle power was really important, but as far as we can tell, it is in later primitive periods that women's power was so very diminished.

Leslie—Why is that?

Irene—There are no easy answers. As we look at those cultures, they were dominated by various ideologies—religious, ethnic, nationalistic. These must have been mostly created by men. Most puzzling, it appears that the women generally agreed on these group fantasies and went along with them, no matter how they devalued the life of their own children.

During a war, it was considered far worse to destroy a respected building or work of art (mostly the creation and work of men) than to destroy people (mostly the creation and work of women). In fact the purpose of the wars was to destroy the soldiers, the human blood sacrifices. If a cathedral or other religious symbols were destroyed in war while the people inside had been incinerated dying a horrible death, it often ended up that there was more concern about the building.

Leslie—So you are saying that in primitive times most women were not pacifists, not workers for peace, even if their own children had to go to fight in wars?

Irene—Yes, the theory and the reality were quite different. The theory was that women were more peaceful and men more warlike, yet the reality was that most women did not strive more toward peace than men, and did not even protect their own children in most situations leading toward war.

This theory that women were more peaceful and men more warlike persisted in those primitive days in spite of the reality that most women supported most wars, and in spite of the fact that the activists of many of the pacifist movements were mostly men. It even persisted in the face of women who were war leaders, such as England's warrior queens Boudica and Margaret Thatcher.

Leslie—Were there many examples of women with such political power?

Irene—No; there were only rare examples of politically powerful women, such as the female pharaohs of ancient Egypt; Hatshepsut reigned for at least 15 years at a time of peace and prosperity. But her name was later removed from the lists of pharaohs by that male-dominated world.

Even near the end of primitive times, when women became more participatory in the political process, received the vote and much better job opportunities, they often joined the group fantasies espousing war violence. It looks as if women as a group needed the human blood sacrifices of war as much as men as a group did.

Leslie—But we learned, in previous lectures, about observational research studies from primitive times which showed that girls and women did tend to be less individually violent than boys and men.

Irene—Yes, there were such studies, completed during the disturbed social environment of primitive times. Back then there also were laboratory studies, reinforcing those perceptions. Brain imaging studies from the primitive times suggested that women as individuals were often more likely to be compassionate toward fellow human beings.[1]

Leslie—Did women act compassionately during primitive times when they were in groups, too?

Irene—There were many examples; one was the Machsom Watch, a unique Israeli women's organization, which maintained shifts at Palestinian/Israeli checkpoints in the West Bank of Palestine to document the suffering and humiliation of the Palestinians, and try to solve their individual problems when they had nowhere else to turn.

But there were also many men who were nurturing and struggled hard politically for peace. Historians do not know whether there were more men or more women in these peace-loving roles; all they know for sure is that the overall groups, which were at least half women, went to war on a regular basis.

Leslie—So what idea did intellectuals of primitive times use to explain their theory that women were more peaceful?

Irene—There were quite a few theories, based on the understanding of the life experiences of women at that time. One prominent theory was that women were less needy then men as far as life and death issues go. Why? Because women experienced life-giving; they experienced omnipotence; they literally had the powers of gods. Women got to play "all powerful creator" during the birth process. This illusion was then reinforced and tested by many years of power over the children while they grew up.

Leslie—But men are just as essential to the creation of human life as women!

Irene—Yes, men's semen was necessary to create life during primitive times—parthenogenesis was not yet known in humans. It also was true that fathers often were involved in the raising of children, but so many of them didn't seem to get even close to the basic satisfaction that the average mother experienced. It was thought that perhaps this was so because the child was literally an extension of her own body. Women also of course became very invested in children because most of them spent so much of their time and energy raising their children.

Leslie—So the theory was that women already had their omnipotent power needs met by child-bearing and child-raising?

Irene—Yes, that's a good way to put it. The theory went that women were supposed to be more peace-loving because they were in closer touch with the process of creation, the process of life itself, a process that war tries to destroy. Yet this theory came up against the reality that most women supported most wars in primitive times. It also did not account for the behavior of women leaders who did not have children; some of them were leaders in peace and tolerance, such as the American social worker Jane Addams who opposed World War I because she was so opposed to violence.[2]

Leslie—So what happened?

Irene—In the world of the primitives, women primarily became supporters of a war by being members of their group. In spite of their own life-affirming personal histories related to children, they usually were no more immune to circulating group fantasies leading toward war than men were. They allowed the product of their life's work—their children—to be put into armies to kill or be killed on behalf of the group.

This is one of the strongest proofs of the overriding appeal of group identity and ideology over all other gender, environmental and genetic predispositions.

Leslie—Those group cultures were certainly powerful!

Irene—We have written documents to help decipher how women as goddesses were viewed by their own cultures during very primitive times, regarding the subject of violence and war. The artifacts tend to fall into two rather different views of women. In both sets of documents, women have power—for good (to help armies) or for bad (to contaminate the group).

Soon after writing began, the polytheistic societies were documented to include female goddesses, and one of those mother figures often was selected as a war goddess. In the ancient Mesopotamian culture of the Middle East, there was Inanna/Ishtar—the goddess of love and war, ancient Egypt had the war goddess Sekmet and the ancient Greek culture had Athena—the goddess of wisdom and war. Although men did the fighting, we can only guess that the female goddesses might have been thought to have determining power in the war playground of life and death.

Leslie—The war playground of life and death?

Irene—Psychologists of primitive times postulated that the feelings about women in their own families by these ancient armies of sons might have been expressed in these powerful mother-figures of war. With these war goddesses, the sons expressed their awe of the mother's power to bestow and sustain life as well as the dangerous fear of their rejection—which can mean death to an infant, just as it can mean death on the battlefield.

Leslie—Today's lecturer was the same one who spoke earlier about purity and violence. Were women special targets of purity taboos in ancient times?

Irene—There are a lot of interesting very ancient artifacts dealing with the subject of purity, including how it applied to women. In the Middle East, the Sumerians, (the initiators of the ancient Mesopotamian civilization and the people who originated writing), had the first written word for being polluted—U.ZUG. The word also meant being temporarily tabooed by the society because a person was unclean. Their successors, the Akkadians, used the Sumerian writing system but applied it to a different language. The Akkadian word for a person under temporary taboo was *musukku*. The Akkadians also had a special word *urrushtu* for a "dirty woman" which applied both to a woman after childbirth and to one who was having her menstrual period.[3]

Just as women became a focus of pollution in ancient Mesopotamia, this purity obsession toward women was continued in many Middle Eastern and other societies for a very long time. Often the natural functions of women became the living symbols of impurity for their group. After all, women do go through an *urrushtu* period. During such occasions in ancient Mesopotamia, they would enter a temporary tabooed state. A later example are the strict so-called *Niddah* rules set up by the Jewish Talmud regarding a menstruating women's sexual behavior and checks for cleanliness.

Leslie—If women were targets of purity taboos, could that help explain why they were so oppressed historically?

Irene—It can be argued that the oppression of women in many societies, which eventually extended to so many areas of their life during later historical times, may have begun with the all-important purity taboo. The sacred Black Stone at the very center of the Muslim religion was "a white sapphire from the Garden, but when menstruating women touched it during the pre-Islamic period, it turned black".[4]

Leslie—How long did the tabooing of women continue historically?

Irene—Even as late as the twentieth century AD, there were pockets of overwhelming fear of women. The fear of even the gaze of an (impure) woman became exaggerated in some interpretations of the religions from the Middle East, ending up with the Moslem Taliban of Afghanistan throwing acid on the face of any woman who appeared in public with part of her face showing. Also during that century, there was an extreme Greek Orthodox Christian sect of monks, whose motto was "Orthodoxy or Death", which not only kept women away from their grounds, but even forbade the presence of female livestock.[5]

Leslie—Well that is pretty crazy; in terms of violence in historical times, women were certainly less scary than men.

Irene—Well to be fair, of course not every woman was on the peaceful side in primitive times. About 7% of women in many primitive societies were killers. At that time, the woman murderer was a source of fascination. Just like the possibilities in male criminals, killers who were females were thought to arise either out of 1) *individual factors*—devastating life circumstances or abnormal brain function of either traumatic or genetic origin or 2) *group factors*—such as an expression of a criminal subculture.

Leslie—With men criminals, sometimes it appears to be both factors.

Irene—With women, too. A historical example where it might have been both factors was the woman, Ulrike Meinhof, who was one of the leaders of the notorious Red Army Faction, known as the Meinhof-Baader gang. This was a group which conducted a series of violent kidnappings and assassinations of members of the West German establishment in the early 1970s AD. After she was finally arrested, she committed suicide. An autopsy of her brain showed serious damage sustained during an operation for a brain tumor when she was 26 years old, raising the question of whether she was suffering from diminished mental capacity because of this brain damage.[6]

Leslie—Did they study women murderers during primitive times?

Irene—Yes, because of the perception of women as nurturers, there was particularly high interest when mothers committed homicide. In one study done in the twenty-first century, a psychiatric disease probably genetic in origin was determined in 85% of the killer mothers, more than half of whom also committed suicide. Most of their victims were their own children under six years of age.[7]

Leslie—But wasn't it very unusual for women to kill on behalf of the group?

Irene—In most of the generations living through primitive times, women generally were rarely direct participants in group violence—the human blood sacrifice rituals of war. Human cultures almost always shaped armies along male gender lines. There is some evidence of warrior women in the Sauromatian culture of 6th—4th century BC north of the Caucasus. But this was the exception to the rule for those early times.

However by the twentieth century AD, women had become part, a small part but nevertheless a part, of most armies, both establishment and revolutionary. There was an ambivalence and debate about excluding them from units in regular armies that were destined for front-line battle; however, it should be noted that a few women struggled hard for the right to become objects of sacrificial ritual (soldiers in the line of fire.)

Leslie—Was there any difference in attitude toward women soldiers between the state armies and the guerrilla groups?

Irene—Twentieth century AD guerrilla groups had much less hesitation about sacrificing females; they used women as front-line soldiers to be sacrificed, as shown by the "Black Widow" female Chechen suicide-bombers.[8] The Tamil Tigers operating in Sri Lanka had the highest percentage of girls or women participating in suicide bombings; a Tamil woman suicide bomber killed the prime minister Rajiv Gandhi of India in 1991 AD.[9]

Leslie—So there was a mixing of the individual abuse of women and the group abuse of women in those primitive societies?

Irene—You raise a very interesting point. It has been argued that women also played a role indirectly in violence in the sense that the forces that oppressed women often were the same forces that led to group violence and war. In primitive times, women sometimes were abused by fathers, husbands, brothers, sons and the violence-dominated group culture around them; many more wives were physically abused than husbands.

Leslie—Why couldn't women stop their own abuse, and in the process, rescue their own societies?

Irene—Sometimes women did stop their own abuse in primitive times, but it was quite difficult because of the primitive cultures. What is much clearer to see is what mothers did when their children were abused. Apparently from time to time when children were abused, the mothers felt helpless. However, since ancient Greek times, there have always been some women who wouldn't go along with such decisions by husbands. In an ancient Greek play, a mother, Clytemnestra, kills her husband Agamemnon in revenge for his murder of their adolescent daughter in a group sacrificial ritual. She doesn't agree with the group's need for human blood sacrifice; she doesn't respect her husband's decision; she punishes him with death himself. But, as the Greek playwrights suggest, killing is no real answer; it continues the cycle of violence; Clytemnestra is then killed by her own son. The ancient Greek women were being taught in such religious plays that violence toward their children, by anyone at all, is unacceptable and sets off a cycle of tragic events. Millennia later, the message still had not been learned by most societies.

CHAPTER 13

▼

WAR SUBSTITUTES FOR THE POWERLESS

Abstract 1013 In the twentieth century, two different types of war substitutes were increasingly developed for groups who were losing their wars and rapidly becoming powerless. For suicide bombers, the rhetoric of extreme hate resulted in forced intermingling of the bodies of bombers and their victims, as in symbolic sex. Everybody died. For those engaging in nonviolent direct action, the rhetoric of loving their enemy was designed to guilt-trip the enemy into feeling hateful and impure. Nobody died.

Leslie—So what did you think of the lecture on the substitutes for war that were used by powerless groups?

Irene—They appeared to be the sacrificial scenarios of the truly desperate.

Leslie—These war substitutes were created by groups that were being deliberately humiliated and feeling defenseless in the face of stronger enemies; they were also used by groups staring at defeat at the end of a conventional war.

I noticed that, just as with war, the ostensible reason for these struggles often was boundaries and power. Tell me more about the two forms of alternative group fighting which existed throughout primitive history and were fine-tuned and formalized during the twentieth century. What was the underlying message that these powerless groups were trying to accomplish?

Irene—These methods were based on extreme ideologies that have been honed by people trying to hold on to their sense of intactness and good identity/purity in spite of their inferior strength. Both used the tactic of trying to make the enemy feel impure to achieve their goals.

Leslie—So they tried to get the enemy to become aware of, to experience, to actually feel, the *depersonalization of the impure* status that these groups were projecting on that enemy?

Irene—You could put it that way. They sent out their very young men to act out the group fantasy; both war substitutes required "soldiers" who had a truly dedicated, unswerving ideology.

Leslie—I was confused by the point that the lecturer made about how the two techniques appeared to be only opposite on the surface .

Irene—Although both techniques were extreme, they appeared to be opposites. In the suicide bomber methodology, <u>everybody died</u>—the warrior and the enemy. Here the rhetoric of extreme HATE was changed in action to the violence of extreme LOVE, a forced intermingling of the bodies of both groups.

In the second methodology, that of nonviolent direct action, <u>nobody died</u>—not the warriors, although they might have gotten beaten up, and not the enemy. Here the rhetoric of professed LOVE of the enemy is combined with an aggression that carefully eschews violence designed to denigrate the enemy [make them feel HATEful] when confronted with superior purity.

Leslie—Tell me more about suicide bomber programs, like those staring at defeat at the end of a conventional war.

Irene—These suicide bomber acts tried to make sure <u>everybody died</u>. These programs were often combined with more conventional killing of the enemy. During the last stages of World War II, the Japanese developed "divine wind" programs which included *kamikaze* dive bombers, *kitin* submarines full of explosives with martyrs inside to direct them, and flying suicidal *oka* rockets. The *kamikase* pilots were later glorified as great, willing martyrs for the emperor. Actually they "were sheep at a slaughter-house. Everybody was looking down and tottering. Some were unable to stand up and were carried and pushed into the plane by maintenance soldiers." [1]

Leslie—So these groups were feeling so humiliated and defenseless in the face of a stronger enemy, that they initiated suicide bombing?

Irene—Yes; a good example of that kind of suicide bombing occurred with the Liberation Tigers of Tamil Eelam in Sri Lanka. The fight inside Sri Lanka for a homeland for the Tamil people by the Liberation Tigers of Tamil Eelam resulted in a very bloody civil war in the twentieth and twenty-first centuries. Suicide bombers killed the president of Sri Lanka and the son of Indira Gandhi of India; they decimated Sri Lanka's political and intellectual leadership killing government ministers, mayors and moderate Tamil leaders. [2] The head of the Sea Tigers, Soosai, boasted that the attack in Yemen on the U.S. warship, the Cole, had been copied by Al Quaeda (another group sending out suicide bombers) from the earlier suicide destruction of one third of the Sri Lankan Navy by the Sea Tigers.

Leslie—What about the martyr [*shahid*] programs of Islamic fundamentalists in the Arab world?

Irene—By the turn of the century at 2000 AD, the Tigers had sent out more than three times as many suicide bombers, including children, as an Islamic fundamentalist group such as Hamas. [3] However the Islamic fundamentalists also were ruthlessly exploitive. The "black widows" of the Islamic Chechen secessionist movement have been reported to be sometimes recruited by being raped and left with public shame so that their future was taken away. [4] The rape psychologically foreshadowed their mission.

Leslie—So leadership that created these programs had no mercy at all, no chance for survival, of their own women and children?

Irene—In these situations there was no element of chance for survival for these soldiers; this was an extreme, absolute commitment. For example, to be sure that the combatants die, the suicide warriors of the Liberation Tigers of Tamil Eelam carried cyanide capsules on their persons.

Leslie—Did these kind of programs bring results?

Irene—Although the rhetoric is of intense hate, in fact the actions of suicide bombers are reminiscent of intense sexual love—the bombers forcibly embed their own body parts into the bodies of their enemy. Such desperate rape-like techniques have a poor record of winning a group struggle; they tend to make their enemy feel violated, impure and more determined than ever never to give in. If the goal of peace is ever achieved, it tends to be imposed by outside forces on two very bitter, apparently irreconcilable, groups.

Leslie—Do the nonviolent direct action techniques have the same poor record?

Irene—The historical record for success by nonviolent direct actions is somewhat better than the record for suicide bombing. Nonviolent direct actions also were extreme but opposite events where nobody died. In the nineteenth century, Henry David Thoreau used this technique in the United States—he went to jail rather than support the Mexican War by paying the state poll tax. In the twentieth century, these forms of direct action were developed in greater detail by Mahatma Gandhi in India. The nonviolent soldiers used their own bodies but carried no weapons of violence as they walked, stood or sat on behalf of their cause without threatening their opponent. The enemy rarely killed them because they posed no physical threat at all. The threat was psychological only; they were trying to induce guilt. Here the rhetoric was of love, supposedly love for the misguided enemy group, yet the action was specifically designed to humiliate that enemy by making them feel hateful and impure.

Leslie—Was Gandhi a brilliant man?

Irene—Undoubtedly, but it was the power of his human values that was his strength. In fact, he said that the thing he feared most was the hard heart of the intellectuals.

Leslie—Give me examples of some nonviolent direct actions in the twentieth century:

Irene—Although most people scoffed at nonviolent techniques during primitive times, there were a few limited successful actions, as follows:

-in 1929, an army of up to 80,000 very poor Muslims, known for their violent Pathan culture, took pledges and remained nonviolent in the face of extreme repression by British police in northwest colonial India.[5] Even Gandhi said the turnabout of this Islamic army was "almost like a fairy tale."
-on March 6, 1943 nonviolent tactics rescued 1735 Jewish people from being sent from Berlin to their deaths in the concentration camps because of the famous Rosenstrasse protest by their non-Jewish relatives and other Berlin supporters. That was the day, in the midst of World War II, that Goebbels—the *Gauleiter* of Berlin—ordered the SS not to kill the German nonviolent demonstrators and to give in to their demands.[6]
-in 1947, the British lost their most profitable colony [India] in their empire at least in part because of the nonviolent tactics of Gandhi.
-in 2000, at the end of the Balkan wars, Milosevic was ousted as president of Serbia without the shedding of human blood largely because a key element of the peaceful revolution was planning in advance by a group of nonviolence resisters called Otpor. This group was trained by Gene Sharp, the famous author of the "bible" of nonviolence.[7] As one of the leaders of Otpor named Srida said: "We would like to be in the encyclopedia of nonviolence resistance with Gandhi and Martin Luther King."

Leslie—I am not clear about nonviolent direct action and pacifism—are they the same?

Irene—In primitive times, pacifism was not the same phenomenon as Gandhian nonviolent direct action. It's true that the word "pacifism" was used as a shorthand for any form of opposition to violence and war, but it had a more specific meaning.

Leslie—Which was?

Irene—Pacifism was defined as the other side of the coin of war, and was directly related to war itself, as a strong reaction against it. Pacifism often becomes a political force during the "dance of death phase" before a war got touched off. Pacifism favored a solution by diplomatic accommodation, even appeasement, keeping the status quo from changing, in a situation where war is in the air. Such pacifists often do not have a life-commitment against all war killing; they can quickly become soldiers of violence. In the antebellum North before the American Civil War, the apparently sincere pacifism of the abolitionists disappeared overnight when the first killing of the war took place at Fort Sumter in Charleston Harbor; they were among the first to volunteer for the Union Army. Before World War II, a large group of English pacifists who had been traumatized by the horrible losses of World War I gave up their pacifism as soon as Hitler invaded Poland.

Leslie—OK; I have some nonviolent resistance to any more learning today.

Irene—Fine, tomorrow we take a look at the surprising historical fact that there actually were societies without war in primitive times.

▼

CHAPTER 14

ABANDONING WAR BY THE POWERFUL

Abstract 1014 During primitive times, war was not an obligate or inevitable group activity as shown by the various groups who gradually and consciously eschewed war. Examples ranged from head-hunters (such as the Kwakiutl-speaking native Americans) to industrialized European societies (such as Sweden). These societies avoided the human blood sacrifice of war by substituting alternative nonlethal forms of human sacrifice.

Leslie—I suppose that this lecture might have been called the "exceptions to the rule" lecture, because it was about the few societies in primitive times who actually gave up both individual murder (capital punishment) and mass murder (war).

Irene—Yes, that's a good summary—these were indeed the exceptions to the rule in primitive times.

In American slang of the twentieth century, when a man was murdered, he was "wasted." When he died, his body was simply disposed of (not eaten). Wasted. These nonviolent groups that we are about to review actually taught us a very fundamental lesson about wasting—that, even if there was no violence, it was still necessary to perform some kind of group sacrifices from time to time. A group of people bonded together still needed to "waste" something whenever the society itself went through a crisis. But since these nations without war could no longer tolerate human blood sacrifice, they developed nonlethal forms of sacrifice—what we might call today *economic* or *political wastings.*

Leslie—Let me get this straight. Groups of people, or leaders on their behalf, deliberately wasted all kinds of things from human lives to economic benefits?

Irene—That's right. There were all kinds of variations of wasting—wasting human lives (the bloody form of wasting), simply destroying material goods, giving up those economic goods to other people, deliberately giving up political power, etc.

Leslie—Why all this wasting? I don't get it.

Irene—Well, possibly because all those group sacrifices, those wastings, had the deep psychological benefit of relieving anxious, hidden guilt, somewhat like a penance. The original form of wasting—throwing valuables away, particularly those of human lives—relieves such shared bad feelings in a group. The economic or political wastings further improves the mood of the group by adding another psychological boost on top of the original one—the original relief of guilt (deliberately giving up of valuables) combined with a positive feeling of pride in altruism (sharing of valuables with others).

Leslie—In primitive times, who discovered that principle of nonlethal sacrifice? Was it societies that reached certain levels of industrialization or what?

Irene—No, there actually were many different kinds of societies that developed the nonlethal sacrifices, the kind of *wastings* that prevented war. We might start with <u>The Kwakiutl-speaking American natives</u> and their development of <u>potlatch.</u>

Leslie—I've heard of potlatch; who developed it and what was it?

Irene—Certainly one of the most fascinating findings in all of the anthropological work on war was the story of the fierce Kwakiutl-speaking American natives in the northern Pacific coastal area of North America. They were studied starting in 1792 by newly arrived Europeans, which was the date of the first European contact with them. A number of investigators, Frank Boaz is the best known, created archival textual materials about this group [1]

Leslie—Doesn't "fierce" usually mean orientation toward violence and killing?

Irene—Yes, they started out that way, but during the period under study, warfare slowed down to the killing of fewer and fewer men until, when only one enemy man was killed, that would end each war. Then war was extinguished altogether. At the same time the institution of <u>potlatch</u> (from the Chinook word *patshatl* meaning "to give away") grew and grew.

Leslie—Exactly what does potlatch mean?

Irene—Potlatch refers to the destruction or giving away of property out of rivalry for social prestige. They started out by throwing away their coppers into the sea (very prized possessions made of copper that they created), a kind of beginning intermediate nonlethal activity that was still a complete waste. In 1897, Boaz recorded a statement made during the 18-day winter dance ceremonial that indicated that the Kwakiutl were aware of what they were doing. The statement went as follows:

> We used to fight with bows and arrows, with spears and guns. We robbed each other's blood. But now we fight with this here (pointing to the copper he was holding in his hand), and if we have no coppers, we fight with canoes or blankets. [2]

Leslie—So why did you call them fierce?

Irene—The original Kwakiutl American natives of British Columbia when first studied had wars with weapons of bows, arrows, spears, slings, and clubs. Guns were later added when the Indians first learned about them from Europeans. The Kwakiutl Indians were headhunters.

Leslie—Headhunters!

Irene—A typical war party was often made up of several great canoes carrying from 30 to 50 men apiece. As many as 200 men and sometimes more were in the war party. The Kwakiutl were greatly feared and their warfare appeared to be waged out of a desire to retaliate, or above all to acquire or maintain the prestige of being considered utterly terrifying. This killing was waged on the outnumbered or the unsuspecting. It was ceremonialized for the most part, confined to its season from the middle of August to the first of October. Their methods of war were those of surprise, ambush, and trickery with the objective of killing and taking heads. What actual violence occurred was dramatized superbly and outrageously. The result was that few American native tribes have been more feared.

Leslie—Did they have a word for war?

Irene—The Kwatiutl word for war—*wina*—applied not only to fights between groups, such as tribes or clans, but also to acts of violence on the part of a single individual. It is interesting to note that by the time these Amerindians were being observed by Europeans, their warfare was slowing down to the point that they sometimes would be satisfied with killing only one man for revenge, even though they had a tremendous desire to be known as the most bloodthirsty of all the Indians.

Leslie—But then they gradually changed from being blood-thirsty?

Irene—During the period that they were observed by Europeans, the wars were decreasing but the potlatch ceremony kept increasing. Its purpose was always to affirm or reaffirm social status. The ceremony moved from a destruction of throwing valuable things away in the sea into a ceremonial distribution of property and gifts. It reached its most elaborate development among the southern Kwakiutl from 1849 to 1925. Although each group had its characteristic version, the potlatch had certain general features. Ceremonial formalities were observed in inviting guests, then speechmaking, and then the distribution of goods by the donor according to the social rank of the recipients. The proceedings gave wide publicity to the generosity of the donor and to the social status of the donor's recipients because there were many witnesses. Important events such as births, marriages, deaths, and initiation into secret societies were also occasions for pot-latches.

Leslie—Every community has parties on the occasion of important events; why was this different?

Irene—The potlatch was considered as a kind of fighting, as a kind of competition. As one Kwakiutl said

> "The time of fighting has passed. The fool dancer represents the warriors. But we do not fight with weapons; we fight with property."[(3)]

Leslie—Sounds like a lot of societies we have studied where there were fights over property.

Irene—No, it's not the same. The potlatch gifts were destroyed or given away. That's the key thing. They were forms of sacrificial rites. In fact, the European observers originally misinterpreted the potlatch ceremony as evidence of mental imbalance among the Kwakiutl-speaking natives. They were particularly stunned by very rich chiefs who actually threw their wealth into the sea during potlatch ceremonies.

Leslie—So how did the European observers explain this behavior?

Irene—Psychologists who looked at these records later speculated that the Kwak-iutl warfare was waged out of "feelings of grief and shame rather than for an economic purpose."[(4)]

Leslie—Did any other primitive societies have potlatch?

Irene—Yes, quite a number. Another American native group, the Orinocos of South America, also was believed to have had a form of potlatch.

Leslie—Was there potlatch outside of the Americas?

Irene—On other continents, too. Perhaps what is most fascinating of all about a potlatch ceremony is that it performs its psychopolitical role for the group *even if it is a fake*. Such a sham potlatch was recorded in Afghanistan in 630 AD by a

Chinese pilgrim. The Buddhist king of Baniyam gave away his worldly goods to the monasteries and became destitute in a public ceremony called the *moksha mahaparishad*. However the king's ministers and low-ranking officials afterwards redeemed the valuables from the monks and secretly returned them to the king.[5]

Leslie—Its psychopolitical role being one of a sacrifice on behalf of the group?

Irene—You got it! Do you want to discuss other primitive societies that gave up war?

Leslie—Yes, tell me about such a society on the European/Asian continent.

Irene—How about <u>Sweden</u> where they substituted <u>economic sacrifice</u> to take the place of the blood sacrifice of their young people?

Leslie—O.K.

Irene—Sweden also was a nation with a preceding history of terrible "all-devouring fury", this time by its Viking invaders. Starting around 500 AD, the Pan-Scandinavian Vikings ravaged the parts of Europe accessible by water; their heyday was a period of three centuries between 800 to 1100. These raids were finally halted, not by the groups that they victimized overseas, but by the increasing pressure by government and business enterprises within their own lands.

Leslie—So, like the Kwakiutl-speaking Native Americans, they were a particularly fierce society before they gave up war.

Irene—The reputation of the Viking raiders was terrible. But very gradually Sweden began a process that could be considered an exchange of economic sacrifices for blood sacrifices. Although the killing of wars continued intermittently, in 1570 and again in 1613, the Swedish people paid ransom to Denmark to buy back part of their own country that they lost in war. The financial strain was almost strangling and extraordinary taxation was imposed on the whole country of Sweden; nevertheless apparently the concept of paying for instead of fighting back was developing.

Sweden actually was a winner in its last war with Norway which ended on August 14, 1814. A long-lasting era of peace then began in Sweden which stretched subsequently for a very long time. Earlier that year, the Treaty of Kiel (January 14, 1814) had forced Denmark to cede the territory of Norway to Sweden for which Sweden paid 1 million riksdalers plus Norway's share of the Danish national debt. Sweden meant to "buy" Norway without having to fight for it; but the Norwegians resisted, requiring more bloodshed before the August 14 armistice. However, in spite of having both paid Denmark for the country and fought with the Norwegians, Sweden allowed Norway to become an independent nation without a drop of blood being spilled in 1905.

Leslie—Let me get this straight—not a single Swedish soldier was involved in a war after 1814, even though there were a series of European wars after that date?

Irene—Correct. Starting in 1814, Sweden never again called upon its troops to shed their blood. Individual Swedes did volunteer to fight in neighboring countries (the Finns with the help of Swedish volunteers fought the Russians beginning in 1939). One can not help but conclude that the young soldiers of Sweden were truly beloved by their group, back in primitive times.

Leslie—That's amazing. What happened in Sweden during the big wars of the twentieth century—World War I and World War II?

Irene—When one reads Swedish history, one sees all types of maneuvers by members of the Swedish ruling classes and diplomatic corps enticing Sweden into various alliances which might have resulted in group loss of life. What is interesting in reading this history is how the people as a whole seemed to have blocked attempts at war.

For example, during World War I, a conservative editor, Adrain Molin, appealed to the king not to delay too long in leading Sweden into the war. He said that although the people might seem opposed to involvement, as soon as the troop trains moved, they would be united behind the royal leadership. However, the people on the whole were "undoubtedly more firmly determined in their peace-mindness than Adrain Molin thought."[6]

Leslie—And World War II?

Irene—During World War II, concessions, such as furnishing iron ore to the German war machine, were made in response to Nazi pressure. These concessions included the passage of the German Engelbrecht Division crossing northern Sweden in June 1941 when the war was resumed in Finland. King Gustav, Foreign Minister Gunther and Gosta Bagge, leader of the Conservatives, were all in favor of granting the concession, and it may even be that the king suggested that he might resign if the demands were refused. As much as possible, the concessions were hidden from the public. However, the movement of the German soldiers could not be hidden and there was a very strong popular reaction against the passage of the Germans through Swedish territory.

Leslie—World War II went on four more years; what happened after the 1941 concessions?

Irene—From time to time during World War II, the German invasion forces were reportedly poised to strike at Sweden, but, even so, the Swedes had an almost unanimous consensus on a neutrality policy. Although they remained neutral, the Swedes did help many others during World War II. When the Nazis attempted to round up the Jews of Denmark, Swedes helped about 8,000 Jews escape to Sweden where they and some 7,000 other Danes lived through the later half of the war, many in private homes. From the Baltic states, especially Estonia, some 35,000 refugees fled to Sweden. About 70,000 Finnish children were received in Swedish foster homes.

Leslie—Would you consider these acts as altruistic/economic sacrifices of the Swedish people when the world around them was full of the blood sacrifice of war?

Irene—Very good. There is no doubt that there were many historical, geographical, and economic factors that led Sweden to be able to successfully maneuver itself into a continuing policy of neutrality while Europe was regularly embroiled in wars. Their smaller Scandinavian neighbors—the Danes, the Finns, and the Norwegians—were less successful in staying neutral in these conflicts.

Leslie—So what is the conclusion that one can draw from Swedish history? Was their historical slow process of alternation between war and economic sacrificing relevant?

Irene—Most probably. From our point of view looking back, there was something to be learned about the attitude of the non-elitist people in Sweden about group killing, and the crucial role this group consensus had at several points in the nation's history when the possibility of war hung in the balance. The innumerable social advances of Sweden in the twentieth century were well known and included support for working mothers and fairness to women; this may have contributed to their reluctance to kill their sons. It is possible to conjecture that when Sweden began to use money (economic sacrifices) as a currency on the table along with war, it started moving away from the bloody sacrifice of its young people. The Swedes also gave up capital punishment; they moved out of the killing mode.

Leslie—How about their neighbors; was it a peaceful part of the world?

Irene—To the north of Sweden and Finland lived a hearty people, the Samis formerly known as the Lapps, who had a language related to Finnish and Estonian. These people reported that they were pacific by nature, and one member of their society insisted: "We don't even have a word for war in our language"[7]

Leslie—You said these societies that gave up war were the exception to the rule. Any more exceptions?

Irene—Yes, an interesting exception was <u>Switzerland</u> which was <u>a land of guns and peace</u>. It was a small mountainous country in the center of Europe. Although Switzerland was a country where a number of European pacifist movements were born, it also was a country that had been long known for its mercenary soldiers. Perhaps this became a mechanism for draining off the small subgroup of men present in their society who enjoy violence, because Switzerland also became a society that historically cherished its neutrality during European wars.

Leslie—Maybe with its tall mountains to deter aggressors, that made it possible to be a society that dared to give up war.

Irene—It is interesting to note that Switzerland had the same pattern as the Kwakiutl-speaking Indians when it was ending its wars for good—smaller and smaller number of men being killed. The last war of Switzerland where Swiss soldiers were actually killed during battle action was in 1845, and it was a Catholic—Protestant civil war. Although civil wars usually result in great numbers of national casualties because both sides are from the same country, the Swiss Civil War of 1845 only lasted 25 days and very few soldiers were killed. In retrospect an argument can be made that such a tiny war appears to have signaled that this society was moving beyond war.

Leslie—What happened during World War II, which was swirling all around them?

Irene—Switzerland mobilized a huge army during World War II to deter invasion if necessary, in fact it was never used. The Swiss through the twenty-first century had a standing militia with universal male conscription but they never declared war and remained a peaceful society. It was a society of guns and peace. They also gave up capital punishment.

Leslie—Any more exceptions to the rule—societies without war?

Irene—Let's finish up today with The Amish and their concept of *meidung* Personally I just found fascinating the information about a group of people called the Amish people who eschewed violence.[8] When these people, who really gave up killing in any form, immigrated to the United States from their homeland Germany, their pacifism was put to the extreme test. On Sept 19, 1757, native Americans attacked the house of Jacob Hochstetler, whose farm was in the Northkill area of Pennsylvania. In the evening there was a disturbance, and one of his children opened the door and was shot in the leg by a native American. The child quickly reached for the rifle he used for hunting but his father stopped him, objecting and stating that it was against their principles to take human life, even native American life. The house was then set afire by the native Americans. When the family escaped through the cellar window, the mother, one son, and one daughter were caught and scalped. Jacob and his sons, Joseph and Christian, were later caught and taken captive. After several years of living with the native Americans, they managed to escape. Other Amish families also suffered similar fates.

Leslie—Is that really a true story! Who were these people?

Irene—The Amish originally came to America as part of a much larger movement of Palatinate Germans—other German-speaking people including the Mennonites and other religious groups. Peak immigration of the first wave to America was from 1727-1770, while the second wave of Amish immigration came in the period 1815-1860. Because the Amish came from the religious non-conformists called the Anabaptists, they were persecuted and had been moved around in German–speaking territories. The original Anabaptist movement started in the German-speaking part of Switzerland. Generations later Jacob Ammann, the man who founded the Amish sect, was born in Switzerland and later migrated to Alsace.

Leslie—There were a number of pacifist movements in world history; what was so remarkable about this group?

Irene—This is what is remarkable. Although they came to a country which later had one of the highest rates of murders in the world, yet only one Amish person ever committed a murder in the United States in the hundreds of years that they lived here. This is at least as far as we can determine, although our records do not go much past 2000. Also they refused to participate in the Armed Services, so not a single Amish person ever murdered anyone else under the guise of state sanction.

The Amish lived in many countries, and as far as can be determined, there has only been this one murder in their group since it was founded in over 400 years that we have records. The one exception happened in Pennsylvania when a seriously mentally ill Amish man, Edward Gingerich, murdered his wife during a hallucination in 1993; he cut out her body organs and stacked them in a pile during a wildly psychotic episode. Otherwise not a single Amish person ever committed a murder, either as an individual or as a member of a group. Pretty amazing.

Leslie—Do you have any explanation of how they could prevent almost all killing, even by individuals?

Irene—Some archivists went searching for an explanation of this remarkable achievement, and the original founding documents of this Protestant group suggested a possible answer. The Schleitheim Articles, which determined how they behaved, were issued by a secret conference of Anabaptist leaders in February, 1527. These articles discussed baptism, adultery, rejection of oath, etc. but of greatest interest is Article no. 6, entitled "The Sword." It reads:

> The Sword (government) is an ordering of God, outside the perfection of Christ. It punishes and kills the wicked and protects the good ... Within the perfection of Christ, *only the ban is used* for the admonition and exclusion of

the one who has sinned—without the death of the flesh—simply the warning and the command to sin no more. The rule of the government is according to the flesh; that of Christians, according to the spirit.

Leslie—So the ban was used instead of the sword; is that right?

Irene—Correct—what this article says is that, within their religious community, the custom of banning of a person, who has done an evil deed, is going to take the place of any other kind of punishment.

Leslie—Did it work?

Irene—It appears to have worked quite well. In 1536 a young Catholic priest called Menno Simons joined the Anabaptists and his followers were called "Mennonites." However, in 1693, Jacob Ammann broke from the Mennonites and formed the Amish Party, as it was called, primarily over what he perceived to be a failure of rigid enforcement of the principle of banning and shunning for a person who had done something wrong. This practice of social avoidance was called *Meidung* and the company of the shunned person was to be avoided by all members of the church, including his own family.

The original document was careful to point out that the members must not treat the offenders as an enemy, but exhort them as brethren in order thereby to bring them knowledge of their sins and repentance so that they might again become reconciled to God and the church. By insisting that *Meidung* be very strictly enforced, Jacob Ammann caused a splintering among the Mennonites; those that stayed with him and adhered to very strict shunning became the Amish Party.

Leslie—I guess Jacob Ammann was a very strict man.

Irene—Very strict indeed! Ammann also attached great importance to the wearing of traditional simple clothing. He condemned the trimming of a beard and wearing of fashionable clothing. Although the use of hook and eyes instead of buttons was not part of the initial controversy, it later symbolized the difference between groups when buttons were introduced into European dress. The Mennonites, another Anabaptist group, were the 'Knopfler' (button people) while the Amish were known as "Haftler" (Hook-and-Eyers). Incidentally, it was a big step backward; buttons have been used in human clothing since 3800 B.C.!

Leslie—So the Amish really stuck with *Meidung* and, with the one extreme exception, never ever killed anybody?

Irene—That's what the records show. Just as violence against others was not acceptable in any form, suicide was also taboo. However, there were suicides among the Amish; they were buried outside the cemetery fence to indicate the sinful state of the deceased. In a research study during primitive times, psychiatric epidemiologists researched all suicides for a 100-year period (1880-1980) among the Old Order Amish.[9] Ninety-two percent of the cases were clustered in four primary pedigrees; the authors concluded there must have been a familial genetic component of depressive disease in those families.

Leslie—Are you suggesting that the culture and religious beliefs of one group of people could possibly overcome the relationship between depression and murder found in other populations during primitive times!?

Irene—It is a fact that—with one severely psychotic exception—no Amish person, even the suicides, ever committed a murder, during the period where we have the records.

Leslie—I want to challenge one thing about the Amish and that relates to their highly patriarchal style of life. There was a large literature from primitive times which suggested that patriarchy is related to violence. The thesis was that hierarchy causes violence because hierarchy creates powerlessness, and powerlessness creates victims—sacrificial victims—sooner or later.

Irene—Yet in this matter too, the Amish contradicted the more general observation.

Leslie—So what exactly did we learn from this lecture?

Irene—Well, what we learned was that the Kwakiutl-speaking Indians, the Swedes and the Swiss, to say nothing of the Amish and other long-term pacifist groups, all showed that war was not an obligate or inevitable group activity of *homo sapiens*. This was so even during primitive times.

The most important piece of information that came out of this review was the understanding that these groups could not give up the group sacrificial ritual itself. Instead these societies avoided human blood sacrifice by substituting other forms of human sacrifice, however always nonlethal. It was a revelation!

CHAPTER 15

▼

CONCLUSION

Abstract 1015 Nuclear weapons, with their nuclear waste, were eventually so devastating that the world community was finally forced into considering the possibility of perpetual peace. It took hundreds of years, but the human blood sacrifice of war was finally controlled by substituting other types of human sacrifice, the non-bloody forms, on a systematic basis.

For the socially-sensitive, guilt-programmed species *homo sapiens*, apparently it takes perpetual sacrifice to obtain perpetual peace.

Leslie—So what did the primitives really think of those irenic (pacific) peoples—like the Swedes and all the long-term pacifist groups—in their midst?

Irene—Mostly they were ignored, or belittled, during those bloody primitive times. It was quite hard for most groups to believe that war was not an obligate or inevitable group activity of *homo sapiens*.

Leslie—So how did they explain groups like the Amish?

Irene—The Amish fascinated the thinkers of primitive times who believed that a certain amount of homicide was natural and inevitable. It was not only that the Amish never engaged in the mass murder of war; but also the almost complete lack of killing by individuals for hundreds of years—with only the one exception of wildly disturbed hallucinating man—which challenged their theories of human behavior. There were many religious and secular groups and pacifist organizations all over the world leading a struggle against violence and war during ancient times, yet wars kept reoccurring.

Leslie—Yet someone must have figured it out at some point; in our modern society today there is no war (so far), and mentally abnormal individuals are so restrained from murdering others that it is an exceedingly rare event indeed. How did those pressures of shame and guilt in humans get directed away from killing and war?

Irene—Before I answer that, let me mention that just as no society in primitive times did ever successfully prevented all automurder (suicide), so we also have not solved that problem either in our community; there is still a lot of work to be done.

Leslie—Yes, but we have made a good start. Tell me how did our world community that is dedicated to peace develop.

Irene—Actually the roots of our modern civilization of today arose much earlier than most of us thought. As far as we can tell, the first person to call himself a citizen of the world was early in the fourth century BC, a Greek man called Diogenes.

Leslie—Citizenship of the world is a step in the right direction, but it is different from getting rid of war.

Irene—Yes, of course you're right. However, perpetual peace—of the type we have so far maintained—also was imagined in primitive times by several Europeans. More than two millennia after Diogenes, Abbe St. Pierre imagined a "paix perpétuelle". Earlier Immanuel Kant thought that peace could be achieved by getting rid of totalitarian rulers (they were called monarchs in his day) and having a structure more closely politically sensitive to the general populace.[1]

Leslie—More responsive to the popular will?

Irene—Something like that. But Kant also imagined getting rid of both blood sacrifice and economic sacrifice to achieve such perpetual peace. He was, of course, correct that you have to stop human blood sacrifice to have perpetual peace. But to get rid of other forms of sacrifice, like economic sacrifice, is a very risky, probably unworkable, proposition.

When your goal is to stop human blood sacrifice, the premise of our society is that you have to have many strong, viable substitutes for it.

Leslie—When was our modern form of society first proposed?

Irene—The credit is usually given to a John Keane living in London, England who proposed in 2003 a global civil society [2] not too dissimilar to what we have today.

Leslie—I learned about war in history class. So how did people stop fighting each other?

Irene—It is usually explained that after the type and amount of war sacrifices of the last few centuries of primitive times finally became unacceptable, humankind had simply had enough. It was touch and go for a while, but in the end, we could no longer murder another generation on purpose, no longer constantly tithe ourselves to buy weapons, no longer abandon children to be turned into miniature killers with light-weight guns that 7 year olds can carry, no longer further abase the environment of our countryside with human-created plutonium (^{239}PU) for nuclear weapons with its half-life of 24,100 years.

Leslie—A half-life of 24,100 years!

Irene—Yes! We remember the twentieth century, not just for its horrible wars and genocides, but because that was when the accumulation of radioactive waste began that still haunts us to this day. Their other pollutants from oil and coal—which incidentally harmed the health of their children—were replaced with non-polluting fuels such as solar, wind and hydro when the health consequences became clear. But it was much later than the twentieth century that the consequences of periodic war became impossible to bear, and modern society began.

Leslie—Did this happen gradually or was it very sudden?

Irene—It was a gradual development. For example, during the "cold" war a substitute for bloody sacrifice developed, a process of deliberate economic wasting, as the United States spent gigantic amounts of money on redundant nuclear weapons; these were completely unnecessary in such huge numbers even if it had been decided to blow all humans off the planet. Together with their Dance of Death partner, the Soviet Union, they deliberately "wasted" the wealth of both societies for many decades.

Leslie—Nuclear weapons had already been exploded in Hiroshima and Nagasaki to end World War II, killing so many.

Irene—Nuclear weapons do more than kill; they deeply and irreversibly stain any one in their vicinity. The Japanese individuals who survived Hiroshima and Nagasaki did not call themselves by the Japanese word for "survivors" ostensibly because it might slight the sacred dead who were not able to survive. Instead they invented a new word for themselves—*hibakusha*—which literally means "explosion-affected persons." These people suffered at many different levels including the ever-present danger to their health from the exposure to massive radiation, their rejection as marriage partners due to possible radiation alteration of their genes and their feelings of survivor guilt after the horrors they witnessed.

Leslie—The physicists who developed those weapons must have felt badly afterwards. Of course, they were part of the rise of "civilization" in primitive times, each step of which was associated with the development of more and more lethal weapons.

Irene—Gradually the realization developed that no one, literally no one, can be trusted with such devastating weapons. Harry Truman, who happened to be in the political position to order those first nuclear explosions, was considered by many as a reasonable man and good president. But when he was a solider in Europe during World War I fighting the Germans, this is what Truman wrote home on the day of the Armistice:

> "It is a shame we can't go in and devastate Germany and cut off a few of the Dutch (German) kid's hands and feet and scalp a few of their old men." [3]

Leslie—War really brings out the worst in people! That reminds me, what eventually did happen with nuclear weapons?

Irene—It took a very long time, the nuclear merchants were so powerful, but eventually non-proliferation treaties were negotiated worldwide. It was one of the important steps as we moved toward a society seeking perpetual peace. The first treaty put all nuclear weapons under international supervision in preparation for their decommissioning, and the second treaty set up international control of the production and disposal of fissile materials necessary for nuclear energy and nuclear weapons. Eventually existing nuclear weapons were dismantled and destroyed.

At one point, an international nuclear fuel bank was created, so that countries could get reactor fuel for reactors as needed without making it on their own. But since nuclear reactors are nothing more than dangerous, contaminating ways to boil water to make electricity, they were eventually abandoned and our energy sources today are all the endlessly replaceable sun, wind and hydro.

Leslie—So where did all these treaties lead?

Irene—In primitive times people couldn't even imagine it, but the leadership around the globe eventually came together and finally agreed on a trial solution to the supposedly intractable problem of perpetual peace. The most essential part of the agenda was organized, scheduled and frequent substitutes for human sacrificial blood rituals on all continents—these events are really glorious altruistic rituals.

Leslie—So this is new kind of socially programmed behavior in modern times?

Irene—No, no; substitutes for human bloody sacrifice have been around for a long time. For example, periods of penance every year characterized the successful religions of ancient times. Some of the religions that lasted more than two millennia often had fasting and other forms of personal sacrifice as a repetitive part of their rituals.

Leslie—But we still have individuals who kill.

Irene—Yes, psychopolitical sacrifice and economic sacrifices built into modern cultures can not completely suppress individual psychotic murderers or suicides, but have made the violence of human blood sacrifice in the form of war obsolete.

Leslie—So human beings need perpetual sacrifice to get perpetual peace?

Irene—That's right. Combined with all the other factors that ameliorate group conflict, now we moved into the age of global peace, a community of bonhomie—at least so far. It is based on directing guilt and suppressing shame.

Leslie—Explain what you mean.

Irene—Through evolution, we are born with those feelings of shame and guilt which have become an intricate part of our innate social sensitivity. For example, guilt is so basic to us that sometimes it even bubbles up when we are innocent.

Leslie—What! Complete innocents feel guilt; that doesn't seem right! Give me an example.

Irene—As we already discussed before, this is most clearly seen in the "guilty survivor" situation—after group catastrophes of many deaths or even after one death of a person close to you, when you think "If only I had done this or that." Often innocent survivors feels inappropriate guilt when they have been in the presence of others acting badly.

Leslie—So we do what with these innate shame and guilt feelings in humans?

Irene—We have set up institutions—institutions that specifically direct the guilt into community social altruism, institutions promoting acceptance of others that dampen down situations of shame, institutions that use our collective intelligence to enhance peace. Just like war used to be, peace has to have layers of institutions, too.

Leslie—Name one such institution.

Irene—One of the most effective bureaus turned out to be the International Bureau of the Dance of Death.

Leslie—I have forgotten what it does.

Irene—During troubled times anywhere in the globe, the Bureau of the Dance of Death goes onto high alert, to prevent the buildup toward war. Its members acknowledge, monitor and engage with the participants in hostile political situations that might reach a boiling point. They have the power to prevent military build-ups.

Leslie—Is that enough?

Irene—No; it is strictly a last resort; prevention of the factors leading toward war in the first place is the key. There are endless other techniques besides the scheduled sacrificial rituals of an altruistic nature.

Leslie—Such as?

Irene—We are bonded together as members of the earth community, and careful to avoid civil wars inside that community. Everybody is having a lot of high level fun, excitement and adventure, even space travelers going to the moon on vacation don't get bored during their trip. People having fun together are less likely to want to kill each other.

Leslie—You are being facetious!

Irene—Not completely, but you know very well about the pastiche of peace-loving measures we have, the mechanisms of constant change that are built into our system as individual cultures grow and adapt. For example, we have an elaborate multi-layered system to deal with the competitive aggression between continents. That reminds me; I understand that your team won an international computer game competition last week—congratulations!

Leslie—Should I worry? Will war ever return?

Irene—To be truthful, the history of our species certainly suggests it is probable, in view of the cyclic nature of human group behavior. There was a tendency toward atavistic war regression which appeared at the nadir of each cycle of history. And the most dangerous disease of the human mind, a longing for utopias, will always be with us.

Leslie—Oh.

Irene—But don't be discouraged. With the incredible brain capacity of *homo sapiens* which is still expanding and improving [4][5], there are no guarantees of anything, but there is hope for the future. We have suppressed the war machines and have greatly improved in our treatment of small number of mentally disturbed persons who might have become violent. Now we must stay constantly vigilant.

Leslie—So you think it possible that war might return?

Irene—Unfortunately, it is quite possible that a malignant political leader filled with charisma preaching utopia may still arise someday, and that some group of people would come under his sway. But this is not as likely to happen as in the past because the culture of our modern societies maintain peace by tending to both the material and psychological needs of its citizens, not the least among them the need for non-lethal sacrificial rituals.

Leslie—So what about the potential homicidal leaders, the small percentage of children born at risk for violence and criminality?

Irene—Although we have available a number of scientific laboratory techniques to identify such young children at risk, as a society we have decided not to use them. Among other reasons, they are never 100% predictive because we know that culture tends to override genetics. In any event, we don't believe in labeling a small child, an act which by itself can cause poor results. We know that we don't understand everything; that there are no absolutes, including hard science.

Instead, as you know, we have set up a civil society dealing with genuine human needs and work with behavior problems as they arise. So far it has worked.

Leslie—So finally to go back to what we were discussing at the very beginning of this symposium, during primitive times, was war the means to an end (specific goals) or was war an end in itself?

Irene—The end.

Bibliography

Chapter One

1—Potts DT (1999) <u>The Archeology of Elam</u>. Cambridge University Press: Cambridge.

2—Wilford JN (2007) Ruins in northern Syria bear the scars of a city's final battle. <u>The New York Times</u>, Jan 16, 2007, p F2.

3—Hall WW, Simpson WK (1971) <u>The Ancient Near East: a history</u>. Harcourt Brace Jovanovich Publishers: New York.

4—Dunlop Nic (2005) <u>The Lost Executioner</u>. New York: Walker & Co.

Chapter Two

1—<u>Rilling J</u>, <u>Gutman D</u>, <u>Zeh T</u>, <u>Pagnoni G</u>, <u>Berns G</u>, <u>Kilts C</u> (2002) . A neural basis for social cooperation. <u>Neuron.</u>35(2):395-405.

2—Saxe R (2006) Uniquely human social cognition. <u>Current Opinion in Neurobiology</u> 16:235-239.

3—Nelson RJ (2005) <u>Biology of Aggression</u>. Oxford University Press.

4—Goldstein, Richard (2001) 'Bertie Felstead, 106, Soldier who joined a time-out in war.' Obituaries, <u>The New York Times</u>, page B6.

5—Ridley, Matt (2003) <u>Nature via Nurture: genes, experience and what makes us human.</u> New York:Harper Collins.

6—Moll J, Zahn R, de Oliveira-Souza R, Krueger F, Grafman (2005) Opinion: the neural basis of human moral cognition. Nature Reviews Neuroscience. 6(10):799-809.

7—Deeley Q, Daly E, Surguladze S, Tunstall N, Mezey G, Beer D, Ambikapathy A,Robertson D, Giampietro V, Brammer MJ, Clarke A, Dowsett J, Fahy T, Phillips ML, Murphy DG. (2006) Facial emotion processing in criminal psychopathy. Preliminary functional magnetic resonance imaging study. British Journal of Psychiatry.,189:533-539.

8—Eronen M, Hakola P, Tiihonen J. (1996) Mental disorders and homicidal behavior in Finland. Archives of General Psychiatry. 53(6):497-501.

9—Kiehl KA, Smith AM, Hare RD, Mendrek A, Forster BB, Brink J, Liddle PF. (2001) Limbic abnormalities in affective processing by criminal psychopaths as revealed by functional magnetic resonance imaging. Biological Psychiatry. 50(9):677-684.

10—Soderstrom H, Hultin L, Tullberg M, Wikkelso C, Ekholm S, Forsman A. (2002) Reduced frontotemporal perfusion in psychopathic personality. Psychiatric Research 114(2):81-94.

11—Soderstrom H, Sjodin AK, Carlstedt A, Forsman A (2004) Adult psychopathic personality with childhood-onset hyperactivity and conduct disorder: a central problem constellation in forensic psychiatry. Psychiatric Research. 121(3):271-280.

12—Bondy B, Buettner A, Zill P (2006) Genetics of suicide. Molecular Psychiatry. 11(4):336-351.

13—Edgar PF, Hooper AJ, Poa NR, Burnett JR (2007) Violent behavior associated with hypocholesterolemia due to a novel APOB gene mutation. Molecular Psychiatry 12:258-263.

14—New AS, Hazlett EA, Buchsbaum MS, Goodman M, Reynolds D, Mitropoulou V, Sprung L, Shaw RB Jr, Koenigsberg H, Platholi J, Silverman J, Siever LJ. (2002) Blunted prefrontal cortical 18fluorodeoxyglucose positron emission tomography response to meta-chlorophenylpiperazine in impulsive aggression. <u>Archives of General Psychiatry</u> 59(7):621-629.

15—<u>Meyer-Lindenberg A</u>, <u>Buckholtz JW</u>, <u>Kolachana B</u>, <u>Hariri AR</u>, <u>Pezawas L</u>, <u>Blasi G</u>, <u>Wabnitz A</u>, <u>Honea R</u>, <u>Verchinski B</u>, <u>Callicott JH</u>, <u>Egan M</u>, <u>Mattay V</u>, <u>Weinberger DR</u> (2006) Neural mechanisms of genetic risk for impulsivity and violence in humans. <u>Proceedings of the National Academy of Science U S A.</u> 103:6269-6274.

16—Caspi A, <u>McClay J</u>, <u>Moffitt TE</u>, <u>Mill J</u>, <u>Martin J</u>, <u>Craig IW</u>, <u>Taylor A</u>, <u>Poulton R</u>. (2002) Role of genotype in the cycle of violence in maltreated children. <u>Science</u> 297:851-854.

17—Miedzian M (1991) <u>Boys will be Boys: Breaking the link between masculinity and violence</u>. New York: Doubleday.

18—Bizot F (2003) <u>The Gate</u>. New York: Alfred A Knopf.

19—Dunlop, Nic (2005) <u>The Lost Executioner: A journey to the heart of the killing fields</u>. New York: Walker & Co.

20—Courtois S, Werth N, Panné J-L, Paczlowski A, Bartosek K, Margolin J-L (1997) <u>Le Livre Noir de Communisme: Crimes, terreur, repression</u>. Paris: Editions Robert Laffont, S.A.

21—Walker, HA (1976) Incidence of minor physical anomalies in autistic patients. In Coleman M (ed) <u>The Autistic Syndromes</u>. Amsterdam: North-Holland Publishing Co.

Chapter Three

1—Volkan, Vamik (2004) <u>Blind Trust: Large groups and their leaders in times of crisis and terror</u>. Charlottesville, Virginia: Pitchstone Publishing.

2—Freud (1921) Group psychology and the analysis of the ego. <u>The Standard Edition of the Complete Psychological Works of Sigmund Freud</u>. (James Strachey, translator) 18:63-143. London: Hogarth Press., 1955.

3—Goldberg, E. (2001) <u>The Executive Brain: frontal lobes and the civilized mind.</u> New York: Oxford University Press.

4—Gonen, Jay Y (2000) <u>The Roots of Nazi Psychology; Hitler's utopian barbarism.</u> The University Press of Kentucky.

5—Lustick, I (1993) <u>Unsettled states: Britain and Ireland, France and Algeria, Israel and the WestBank-Gaza.</u> Ithica, New York: Cornell University Press.

6—Coleman, Mary (1993) 'Human Sacrifice in Bosnia.' <u>The Journal of Psychohistory</u> 21:157-169.

7—Volkan Vamik (1994) <u>The Need to have Enemies and Allies</u> Jason Aronson Publications.

8—Levi, Primo (1986) <u>I sommersi e I salvati (The Drowned and the Saved).</u> Torino: Giuli Eianudi editore s.p.a.

9—Rudolph Binion, personal communication

Chapter Four

1—Michalowski, Piotr (1989) <u>The Lamentation over the Destruction of Sumer and Ur.</u> Eisenbrauns publisher.

2—Power S (2001) 'Bystanders to Genocide: why the United States let the Rowandan tragedy happen.' <u>The Atlantic Monthly</u>, September, pp 84-108.

3—Coleman Mary (1993) 'Human sacrifice in Bosnia.' <u>The Journal of Psychohistory</u> 21:157-169.

4—Stein HF, Neiderland WG (1989) <u>Maps from the Mind; Readings in Psychogeography.</u> Univ. of Oklahoma Press.

5—Persico, Joseph E (2004) <u>11th Month, 11th Day, 11th Hour: Armistice Day, 1918.</u> New York: Random House.

6—Fraser, Antonia (1973) <u>Cromwell.</u> New York: Alfred A. Knopf.

Chapter Five

1—Simeon D, Guralnik O, Hazlett EA, Spiegel-Cohen J, Hollander E, Buchsbaum MS. (2000) Feeling unreal: a PET study of depersonalization disorder. Am J Psychiatry.157(11):1782-1788.

2—Binion, Rudolph (1981) Soundings: psychohistorical and psycholiterary. New York: Psychohistory Press publishers.

3—The sacrificial quotient is discussed in greater detail in Chapter 7.

4—Beisel, David (2003) The Suicidal Embrace: Hitler, the Allies and the origins of the Second World War. Nyack, New York: Circumstantial Books.

Chapter Six

1—Allen, M (1983) Animals in American Literature Champaign, Illinois: University of Illinois Press.

2—Ghigliere, MP (1988) East of the Mountains of the Moon: Chimpanzee Society in the African Rain Forest. New York: The Free Press.

3—de Waal FBM (Ed) (2002) Tree of Origin: what primate behavior can tell us about human social evolution. Harvard University Press.

4—Hogue, CL (1972) The Armies of the Ant. New York: World Publishing.

5—Richardson, Lewis F (1975) Statistics of Deadly Quarrels. third printing. (Eds) Wright, Q & Lienau, CC Pacific Press, California: The Boxwood Press.

6—Mesulam, M-M (2002) 'The human frontal lobes: transcending the default mode through contingent encoding.' Struss DT, Knight RT (Eds) Principles of Frontal Lobe Function. Oxford: Oxford University Press.

7—Kluger, H (2001) Still Alive: a Holocaust Girlhood Remembered. (first English-language edition). New York: The Feminist Press at The City university of New York.

8—Binion, R (1995) Freud ber Aggression and Tod. Pincus Verlag

9—Szaluta, J (1999) Psychohistory: Theory and Practice. New York: Peter Lang.

10—Volkan, V (2004) Blind Trust: Large groups and their leaders in times of crisis. Charlottesville, Virginia: Pitchstone Publishing.

11—Walsh M, Scandalis B (1975) 'Institutionalized forms of intergenerational male aggression.' War, its Causes and Correlates. The Hague: Mouton Publishers.

12—Fornari, Franco (1974) [translator Pffeifer, A] The Psychoanalysis of War. Garden City, New York: Anchor Books.

13—Horney, K (1967) 'The flight from womanhood.' Feminine Psychology. New York: Norton.

Chapter Seven

1—Thomsen, Marie-Louise (1984) The Sumerian Language. Copenhagen: Akademisk Forlag.

2—Tierney, Patrick (1989) The Highest Alter: Unveiling the Mystery of Human Sacrifice. New York: Penguin Books.

3. Shame societies and guilt societies with their collective shame/guilt variables are discussed in Chapter 10.

4—Dunlop, Nic (2005) The Lost Executioner: A journey to the heart of the killing fields. New York; Walker & Co. The Khmer Rouge anthem (Chapter 1) is reprinted with the permission of Walker and Co.

5—Burkert, Walter (1983) Homo Necans. The Anthropology of Ancient Greek Sacrificial Ritual and Myth. Berkeley: University of California Press.

6—Sagan, Eli (1974) Cannibalism: Human Aggression and Cultural Form. New York: Psychohistory Press.

7—Binion, Rudolph (1981) Soundings: Psychohistorical und Psycholiterary. New York: Psychohistory Press.

8—Lotto, David (2002) 'The psychohistory of sacrifice.' (Eds) Piven J, Boyd C, Lawton H <u>Jihad and Sacred Vengeance: psychological undercurrents of history</u>. New York:iUniverse.

9—Maccoby, Hyam (1982) <u>The Sacred Executioner: human sacrifice and the legacy of guilt</u>. New York: Thames and Hudson.

10—Girard, René (1972) <u>Violence and the Sacred</u>. Baltimore: The Johns Hopkins Press.

11—Brooke, James (2002) 'A province celebrates Karzai's narrow escape.' <u>The New York Times</u>, September 7, page A 7.

12—George, Andrew (1999) <u>The Epic of Gilgamesh; a new translation</u>. New York: Barnes & Noble Books.

13—Gonen, Jay Y (2000) <u>The Roots of Nazi Psychology: Hitler's Utopian Barbarism</u>. Lexington, Kentucky: The University Press of Kentucky.

14—Hillberg, Raul (1985) <u>The Destruction of the European Jews</u>. Vol III. New York: Holmes & Meier.

15—Banerjee, Neela (2003) A keeper of secrets now opens up about Iraq's dead. <u>The New York Times</u>, July 29.

Chapter Eight

1 Hillberg, Raul (1985) <u>The Destruction of the European Jews</u>. Vol. III. New York: Holmes & Meier, page 1002.

2—Maccoby, Hyam (1982) <u>The Sacred Executioner: human sacrifice and the legacy of guilt</u>. New York: Thames & Hudson.

3—Lewis, Dorothy (1998) <u>Guilty by Reason of Insanity</u>. New York: Fawcett Columbine.

4—Gonen, Jay Y (2000) <u>The Roots of Nazi Psychology: Hitler's utopian barbarism</u>. Lexington, Kentucky: The University Press of Kentucky.

5—Craig, Gordon (1982) <u>The Germans</u>. New York; New American Library.

6—Gonen, Jay Y (1975) <u>A Psychohistory of Zionism</u>. New York: Mason/Charter.

7—Angiers, Carol (2002) <u>The Double Bond; Primo Levi, a biography</u> New York: Farrar, Straus & Giroux, p. 649.

8—Landesman P (2002) 'A woman's work.' The New York Times Magazine, Sept 15.

9—Milton, John (1648) <u>The Tenure of Kings and Magistrates: Proving that it is lawful, and hath been Held so through All Ages, for Any, who have the Power, to Call to Account a Tyrant or Wicked King, and after Due conviction to depose and put him to death.</u>

10—Stern, Paul C (1995) 'Why do people sacrifice for their nation?' <u>Political Psychology 16: 217-253.</u>

<u>Chapter Nine</u>

1—Lifton, Robert Jay (2000) <u>Destroying the World to Save it: Aum Shinriko, apocalyptic violence and the new global terrorism</u>. New York: Henry Holt Books.

2—Hasler G, LaSalle-Ricci VH, Ronquillo JG, Crawley SA, Cochran LW, Kazuba D, Greenberg BD, Murphy DL (2005) Obsessive-compulsive disorder symptom dimensions show specific relationships to psychiatric comorbidity. <u>Psychiatric Research</u> 135:121-132.

3—Dugger, C (2002) 'India police kill two tied to Calcutta attack.' <u>The New York Times International</u>, January 29.

4—Courtois, S, Werth N, Panne, J-L, Paczkowski, A, Bartosek, K, Margolin, J-L (1997) <u>Le Livre Noir de Comminisme: Crimes, terreur, repression</u>. Paris:Robert Laffont.

5—Miller, Helen H (1938) <u>George Mason: Constitutionalist</u>. Boston: Harvard University.

6—Cotterell, Arthur (1981) <u>The First Emperor of China; the greatest archeological find of our times.</u> New York: Holt, Rinehart and Winston.

7—Menard,L. (2001) <u>The Metaphysical Club</u>. New York; Farrar, Straus and Giroux.

8—Crowe, David and Kolsti, John (1999) <u>The Gypsies of Eastern Europe</u>. Armonk, New York: M.E. Sharpe, Inc.

9—Margolis J (1995) <u>T S Eliot's Intellectual Development</u>. Chicago: University of Chicago Press.

10—McNeil Jr., DG (2002) 'Between voting days, Le Pen's fiery image returned to the spotlight.' <u>The New York Times International</u>, p. A8.

11—Keneally, T. (1982) <u>Schindler's List</u>. Serpentine Publishing Company PTY Ltd.

Chapter Ten

1—Moll J, Zahn R, de Oliveira-Souza R, Krueger F, Grafman J (2005) Opinion: The neural basis of moral cognition. <u>Nature Reviews Neuroscience</u> 6:799-809.

2—Gilbert P (1997) The evolution of social attractiveness and its role in shame, humiliation, guilt and therapy. <u>British Journal of Medical Psychology</u> 70:113-147.

3—Kiehl KA et al. (2001) Limbic abnormalities in affective processing by criminal psychopaths as revealed by functional magnetic resonance imaging. <u>Biological Psychiatry</u> 50:677-684.

4—Soderstrom H et al. (2002) Reduced frontotemporal perfusion in psychopathic personality. <u>Psychiatric Research</u> 114:81-94.

5—Gilligan J (2001) <u>Preventing Violence</u>. New York:Thames & Hudson.

6—Coleman M (1985) Shame; a powerful underlying factor in violence and war. Journal of Psychoanalytic Anthropology 8:67-79.

7—Singer, Milton B (1953) 'Shame cultures and guilt cultures.' Piers G, Singer M (Eds.) Shame and Guilt Springfield, Illinois: Charles C. Thomas publisher.

8—Levy, Primo (1986) I sommersi e I salvati (The Drowned and the Saved) Torina: Giuli Eianudi editore s.p.a.

9—Chivers CJ (2007) 'Dutch soldiers stress restraint in Afghanistan.' The New York Times, April 6, 2007, page A1.

10—Marinetti FT (Feb. 20, 1909) The Founding and Manifesto of Futurism. Le Figaro (Paris).

Chapter Eleven

1—Moffit TE, Caspi A, Rutter M, Silva P (2001) Sex Differences in Antisocial Behavior: Conduct disorder, delinquency and violence in the Dunedin longitudinal study. Cambridge, England: Cambridge University Press.

2—Kovel, J. (1983) Against the State of Nuclear Terror. Boston: South End Press.

3—Pomar J (1981) 'Relacion de Tezxoxo'. Icarbalceto JG (Ed) Nueva Collecion de Documentos para Historia de Mexico. Vol III nendein, Liechtenstein: Kraus Reprints.

4—Shatan, CF (1989) 'Happiness is a warm gun; militarized mourning and ceremonial vengeance.' Vietnam Generation, vol.1, pp127-151.

5—Gilbert M (1989) The Second World War: a complete history. Henry Holt: New York.

6—Farmer S (1999) Martyred Village: commemorating the 1944 massacre at Oradour-sur-Glane. Berkeley, California: University of California Press.

7—Broyles, Jr. W (1984) "Why men love war". Esquire 102:56-61.

8—Sontag, D (2007) 'Injured in Iraq, a soldier is shattered at home.' The New York Times April 5, page A1.

9—Ransohoff R (2001) 'Men's deeply repressed envy of women's ability to create life.' (Eds) Piven, J & Lawton, HW Psychological Undercurrents of History San Jose/New York: Authors Choice Press.

10—Maccoby, Hyam (1982) The Sacred Executioner: Human sacrifice and the legacy of guilt. New York: Thames and Hudson.

11—Dao J (2002) 'Word for Word/the Dirty War.' The New York Times, August 25.

12—Galtieri, Leopoldo obituary (2003) The New York Times, January 13.

13—Sciolino E, Daly E (2002) 'Spaniards at last confront the ghost of Franco.' The New York Times, November 11, p A3.

Chapter Twelve

1—Singer T, Seymour B, O'Doherty JP, Stephan KE, Dolan RJ, Frith CD (2006) Empathic neural responses are modulated by the perceived fairness of others. Nature 439:466-9.

2—Menard L (2001) The Metaphysical Club. New York: Farrar, Straus and Giroux.

3—Stol M (2000) Birth in Babylonia and the Bible. Groningen, The Netherlands: Styx Publications.

4—Inamdar SC (2001) Muhammad and the Rise of Islam. Madison, Connecticut: Psychosocial Press.

5—Bruni F (2003) 'Greek monks guard faith and sacred ground.' The New York Times International, Feb 8, p A3.

6—Landler M (2002) 'German radical's daughter seeks brain kept after suicide.' The New York Times, November 12, p A8.

7—Bourget D, Gagne P (2002) 'Maternal filicide in Quebec.' Journal of the American Academy of Psychiatry and Law 30: 352-354.

8—Chivers, CJ (2002) 'Palestinian militant group says it will limit bombings.' The New York Times International, April 23, p A13.

9—Goldstein JS (2001) War and Gender: How gender shapes the war system and vice versa. New York: Cambridge University Press.

Chapter Thirteen

1—Onishi, Norimitsu (2006) 'Shadow shogun steps into light, to change Japan.' The New York Times International, Feb. 11. p A4.

2—Waldman A (2003) 'Masters of suicide bombing; Tamil guerrillas of Sri Lanka.' The New York Times International, January 14, p A1.

3—Dugger C (2002) 'After ferocious fighting, Sri Lanka struggles with peace.' The New York Times International, April 9.

4—Myers, SL (2003) 'Female suicide bombers unnerve Russians.' The New York Times, August 7, pp A1, A6.

5—Easwaran E (1999) Nonviolent Soldier of Islam: Bodshah Khan, a man to match his mountains. 2nd edition. Tomalse, California: Nilgiri Press.

6—Johnson EA (1999) Nazi Terror; The Gestapo, Jews and ordinary Germans. New York: Basic Books, p 424.

7—Sharp, Gene (1973) The Politics of Nonviolent Action three volumes. Boston, Massachusetts: Porter Sargent Publishers.

Chapter Fourteen

1—Boaz, Franz (1887) 'Census and Reserves of the Kwakiutl Nation.' American Geographical Society vol 19, no. 3.

2—Boaz, Franz (1897) 'The Social Organization and the Secret Societies of the Kwakiutl Indians.' Report of the U.S National Museum for 1895, Washington DC.

3—Codere, Helen (1972) <u>Fighting with Property: A Study of Kwakiutl Potlatching and Warfare—1792-1930</u>. Seattle: University of Washington Press.

4—Drucker P, Heinz RF (1967) <u>To make my Name Good: A reexamination of the Southern Kwakiutl Potlach.</u> Berkeley: University of California Press.

5—Huntington JC (2001) 'The Buddhas of Baniyam.' <u>Archeological Odyssey</u>, July/August issue.

6—Scott FD (1977) <u>Sweden: the nation's history</u>. Minneapolis; University of Minnesota Press.

7—Hoge W (2001) 'Inside the Arctic Circle, an ancient people emerge.' <u>The New York Times International</u>, March 18.

8—Hostetler, J (1964) <u>Amish Society</u> Johns Hopkins Press.

9—Egeland JA, Sussex JN (1985) Suicide and family loading for affective disorders. <u>Journal of the American Medical Association</u>. 254: 915-918.

Chapter Fifteen

1—Kant, Immanuel (1795) <u>Perpetual Peace: A Philosophical Sketch</u>—an essay written in the form of a peace treaty. Translation M. Campbell Smith (1992: reprint of the original English edition of the 1903) Bristol:Thoemmes.

2—Keane, John (2003) <u>Global Civil Society</u>. Cambridge: Cambridge University Press.

3—Persico, Joseph E (2004) <u>11th month, 11th day, 11the hour: Armistice Day, 1918</u> New York: Random House.

4—Mekel-Bobrov N, Gilbert SL, Evans PD, Vallender EJ, Anderson JR, Hudson RR, Tishkoff SA, Lahn BT (2005) Ongoing adaptive evolution of ASPM, a brain size determinant in Homo Sapiens. <u>Science</u> 9:1720-2.

5—Evans PD, Mekel-Bobrov N, Vallender EJ, Hudson RR, Lahn BT (2006) Evidence that the adaptive allele of the brain size gene microcephalin introgressed into Homo sapiens from an archaic homo lineage. <u>Proceedings of the National Academy of Science</u>. Nov. 7 [Epub]

Index

Abbe St. Pierre, 142
Abraham and Isaac, 61
Adam and Eve, 109
Addams, Jane, 115
Agamemnon, 120
Afghanistan, 61, 67, 88,94, 131
Aggression, 7, 11, 18, 80
Al-Qaeda, 83, 123
Amish, 136-139, 142
Animals, 39, 40-43
Argentina, 109-110
Armenians, 27
Aristophanes, 104
Athena, 109, 116
Atram-hasis flood story, 62
Australian aborigines, 28
Automurder (suicide), 10, 18, 142, 146
Aztecs, 21, 101-102
Basic training, 8, 105
Blood 62-64
    of the beloved, 4, 65-75
    revolutionary, 4
Body counts, 1, 34, 55, 73
Bosnia, 22
Boudica, 114

Boundaries and power, 29-31, 39, 40, 45
Brains/brain imaging, 43, 91, 114
    abnormal, 9, 16, 37, 148
British Columbia, 129
Buddhism, 61, 77, 132
Bulgaria, 71
Cannibalism, 57-58
Capital punishment, 6, 53, 135, 136
Cambodia/Cambodians, 4, 13, 27, 73, 77
Charismatic leaders, 17, 22
China, 51, 85, 105
Christians/Christianity, 61-62,79,82,117-118, 135
Clytemnestra, 120
Cognitive templates, 21
"Cold" war, 144
Communists/Communist Party, 68, 76, 77, 82, 83-84
Constitution of the United States, 84
Criminals/criminal gangs, 5, 13, 14, 118
Culture, 17, 20, 21, 98, 105, 112, 116
Cuneiform writing, 2, 26, 51

Dance of Death, 35-38, 39, 44, 55, 74, 78, 81, 86, 95, 97
    International Bureau of, 147
Declaration of Independence, 84
Denmark, 93, 132, 133, 134
Depersonalization, 29, 36-37, 86, 88
Depression, 10-11, 16, 17-18, 139
Diogenes, 142
Double Identity Rule, 65, 67-71
Economics, 39, 40, 43-45
Egypt, 109, 114
Empathy, 6-8
Energy sources, 144, 145
England/Britain, 19, 34, 38, 71, 83, 99-100, 114, 125
Epigenetics, 11
Estonia, 134
Finland/Finns, 9, 134, 135
France, 32, 56, 68, 71, 86, 88, 93, 106
Futurists, 96
Gandhi, Mahatma, 92-93, 124-125
Genetics/DNA, 5, 7, 8, 10, 11, 42, 110
Genghis Khan, 98
Genocide, 4, 6, 13,25-29, 63
    Cambodian, 4, 13, 57, 63
    Holocaust, 23, 27, 28, 63, 68-69
    Porajmos, 69
    Rwandan, 27, 63, 70
    territorial versus purity, 28
Germany/Germans, 21, 27, 28, 38, 53, 66-67, 68-70, 87, 106, 125, 133, 134
Greece (ancient), 57, 61, 62, 93, 104, 109, 110, 120
Group psychology, 6, 12, 14, 16-23, 36, 153

Guilt societies, 90-97
Gulf of Tonkin, 97
Gypsies, 68-70, 85
Hamas, 123
Hate, hatred, 4, 29
Hatshepsut, 114
Hebrew language, 68, 109
Hindus, 67
Hiroshima, 144
Hittite god, Kumarbi, 109
Homicidal trio, 14
Homicide/murder, 5-14, 16-17, 101, 137
Hungary, 104
Hussein, Saddam, 63
Ideologies, 12, 13, 45, 46
Incas, 60, 66
Inanna/Ishtar, 116
India, 92, 124, 125
Iraq, 1, 2, 63, 107
Iran (Elam), 1, 2, 3, 71
Islam/Moslems, 79, 82, 83, 95-96, 117, 119, 123, 125
Italy, 70, 96-97, 102-103
Japan, 79, 123, 144
Jews, 27, 28, 63, 76, 68, 69, 82,117, 125, 134
Kant, Immanuel, 142-143
Keane, John, 143
Khmer Rouge, 4, 13,63, 68, 77
Kish, 3
Kwakiutl Indians, 127, 129-131, 135
Laisser-tuer attitude, 5, 8
Lapps (Samis), 135
Machsom Watch, 114
Mandela, Nelson, 93
Mars, 102
Martin Luther King, 61, 125

Mexico, 21

Middle Ages, 83

Monotheism, 109

Moses, 3

Mounds of corpses, 1, 3

Nagasaki, 144

Native Americans/AmericoIndians, 28, 88, 136

Natural-born killers? 5-7, 13-14

Nature via nurture, 8-9

Nazis, 21, 28,53, 63, 66, 76, 68-70, 76, 83, 87, 93, 104, 106, 133

Neanderthals, 103

Netherlands/Holland/Dutch people, 95-96

Neuropsychiatric disorders, 10

New Zealand, 11

Niddah rules, 117

Non-violent direct action, 121, 124-125

Norway, 132, 133, 134

Obsessive-compulsive disorder, 80

Oliver Cromwell, 83

Oliver Wendell Holmes, 85

Olympics, 110

Oradour-sur-Glane, 106

Orinocos, 131

Osama Ben Laden, 79

Otpor, 125

Pacifism/pacifists, 105, 125-126, 135, 137, 141

Pakistan, 94

Palestine, 114

Patriarchy, 139

Peaceperpetual, 141, 142-143, 145

Pen, Jean-Marie, 86

Persian Gulf region, 2, 3

Plutonium, 143

Political science, 39, 40, 45-47

Polytheism, 109

Potlatch, 129-132

Prejudice, 81, 82, 86, 90

Psychogeography, 31

Psychoanalytic theories, 39, 40, 47-49, 108, 109

Psychohistory, 47, 156

Psychopathy, 5, 9, 13-14, 91

Purity, 66, 76-88, 116-117

Radioactive pollution, 30, 141, 143

Regicide, 71

Robespierre, 88

Roman empire, 102-103, 110

Russia/Soviet Union, 32, 37, 127, 133, 144

Rwanda/Rwandans, 27, 63, 70

Sacrificial quotients, 54, 55

Sacrifices/sacrificial rituals 50-64

altruistic, 51, 56, 130-131, 134, 146

perpetual, 141, 146

wasted, 50, 51, 56-58,128, 130

Savants, 14, 148

Schindler, Oscar, 87

Schleitheim Articles, 137-138

Schweitzer, Albert, 98

Sekmet, 116

Serbia, 22, 95-96, 125

Shame societies, 89-95, 96-97

Sharp, Gene, 125

Sierra Leone, 72

Sikhs, 67

Slavery, 84, 86, 90

Soldiers, 31-33, 72-75, 105-108

boy, 32-33, 71, 72

women, 119

Soviet Union/Russia, 32, 37, 73, 133, 144

Sociopathy, 9, 91

Spain, 110

Srebrenica, 95-96

Sri Lanka, 123-124

Stalin, 14, 37

St. Augustine, 96

Suicide (automurder), 10, 18, 29, 142, 146

Suicide bombers, 119, 121-124

Sumerians and Akkadians, 2, 3, 26, 51, 57, 109, 117

Sweden, 127, 132-135, 139

Switzerland, 135-136, 137, 139

Syria, 2, 3

Taliban, 67, 88, 94

Tamil Tigers, 123-124

Tell Hamoukar, 2

Thatcher, Margaret, 114

Thoreau, Henry David, 124

Torture/sadism, 28, 90, 91, 101

Traumatic reliving, 17, 23-24, 58

Truman, Harry, 144-145

T. S. Eliot, 85-86

United Nations, 96

United States, 11, 28, 32, 66

Uruk, 30

Utopias, 77, 78, 84, 148

Violence, 5-24
    by females, 12, 105, 118, 119
    by males, 11-12, 99, 104, 105, 107-108, 109-110

Wars
    as a sacrificial ritual, 19, 25, 26, 28, 33, 44, 50-75
    Catholic-Protestant wars, 135
    Chechen-Russian war, 119
    civil wars, 25, 34, 82, 84, 110, 155
    Indian-Chinese war, 108
    Iraq-Iran wars, 1,2,
    Folkland war, 110
    Sunni-Shia wars, 82
    US-Iraq wars, 91, 107
    US-Vietnamese war, 73, 74, 97, 104
    World War I, 8, 32, 38, 145
    World War II, 4, 8, 12, 36, 70, 93, 97, 106, 123, 133, 134, 136

War substitutes, 121-126, 127-140

Weapons, 9, 32, 71, 143, 144
    nuclear, 141, 143, 144

Weapons control, 145, 147

Yemen, 123

Yiddish language, 68-69

Zeus, 109

978-0-595-46405-0
0-595-46405-X

Printed in the United States
90351LV00006B/144/A

9 780595 464050